I0533492

Fate

by

Sunrise

BY
S. L. MCMULLIN

Book 2 in the *Secrets by Moonlight* saga

Copyright © 2023 by Stephanie L. McMullin

All rights reserved.
No part of this publication may be reproduced, stored
in a retrieval system, or transmitted in any form or by any
means, electronic, mechanical, photocopying recording,
or otherwise, without written permission of the author.

First Edition: July 2023
Printed in the United States of America
ISBN 978-1-960375-02-5
ISBN 978-1-960375-03-2

The characters and events portrayed in this book are
fictitious and a product of the author's imagination.
Any similarities to real persons, living or dead, named
businesses, and incidents are entirely coincidental and
not intended by the author.

If you purchased this book without a cover, you should
be aware that this book is stolen property.
It was reported as "unsold and destroyed" to the
publisher, and neither the author nor the publisher has
received any payment for this "stripped book.

Cover Photo Credit - Michael McInenly

To my siblings; Jeffrie, Kim, Bonnie, and Michael.
Thank you for your love and support and for humoring
my imagination by joining me on so many exhilarating
adventures throughout our childhood! We've been to
the moon and back a million times over without ever
leaving the yard.

Also by S. L. McMullin

Secrets by Moonlight

TABLE OF CONTENTS

Tell Me Why	1
Different	23
A Moment's Peace	45
No More Secrets	67
Trials And Error	86
Too Much Time	107
Company	132
Boys Will Be Boys	145
Never Say Never	163
Heavy Is The Wait	181
Repercussions	204
It Isn't So.	219
Let It Begin.	234
Deception by Nightfall - Sneak Peek	250

CHAPTER 1

Tell Me Why

The subtle scent of lavender triggers the first of my senses. It has a gentle, calming way about it. For a moment, I let the feeling guide me.

As sleep gradually lifts, I am aware of how heavy my body feels—weaker the more awake I become.

Dull at first, the pain in my head subtly builds.

The room is silent. No insects outside clicking or chirping, no sounds coming from inside, no sounds at all.

The eerie stillness is constricting—suffocating in its impenetrability, nothing like how the lavender made me feel.

Slowly, my eyes flutter open, and I am met by a

room of shadowy darkness. Pulled up to my chin is a familiar fluffy blanket with a thick binding and a silky sheet, cold and smooth against my feet—I am home.

But how did I get here? Was it Jamie?

Slowly, I sit up.

Tender to the touch, my cheek is puffy and burns with an inflamed warmth. A soft cloth is wrapped around my head. Trailing it around to the back, I wince when I touch a large, painful, hard lump. The throbbing builds quickly, magnifying in severity the more gravity pushes down on me. Each pulsating pound forces me to remember everything from Brad's violent touch, his powerful, hard hand slapping across my face, and the fear—so much of it that it nearly destroyed me.

They are not all I recall. Marcas' razor-sharp words had cut me so deep I still feel their heartbreaking intensity.

Tears stream down my face as I breathe erratically, clutching my chest, my upper body bouncing as I desperately try to wrangle back the anguish. Head versus heart; I do not know which one torments me more.

Why? Why did any of this have to happen?

I-I can't . . . I can't do this—I need Jamie!

With a trembling hand, I fling back the bedding and put my legs over the side of the bed. Rising slowly, I take a timid step toward the door. The room wobbles under my feet, and I collapse. The end of the bed saves me; I sit back down.

A moment later, a light flicks on behind the closed door. The dim, yellowish glow highlights the floor from the small crack under it, making my eyes sting.

As I listen to the indistinct muffled voices travel through from the other side, an abrupt deep exhale comes from the armchair in the corner by the door. A jolt of panic streaks up my spine as I bite my lower lip to keep from screaming.

Through the muddied darkness, the silhouette of a slumped-over mound of a person slowly comes into view, with their legs stretched out in front, and arms folded over their chest. Yet their face remains concealed from the light.

"Jamie?" I whisper, my voice trembling.

No answer.

"Niall?"

Still nothing.

The voices outside stop just as the door softly creaks open. A light so bright it makes my head pound inundates the room.

Then darkness once more.

"Shae, you're awake!" Jamie whispers, rushing to me. Throwing her arms around me, she holds me tight, her body shaking as she cries. Clinging to her with every ounce of my strength, I give in to the wave of emotions pressing to break free and cry like no one

3

is watching.

"Shhh, it's ok. I got you," Jamie whispers, caressing my back. "You're safe now."

I doubt I will ever feel safe again.

Neither of us lets up for a long while, that is, until the kitchen light flicks on again.

"Hey-hey, it's ok, it's Finn," Jamie whispers when I tense up and pull away.

"Sorry, I didn't mean—" The lights go out again, and a moment later, Sam and Niall join Finn at the door. "We just wanted to make sure you're alright," Finn says hesitantly.

Sniffing, I smile through my sorrow like everything is alright, but it's not, nowhere near it.

Though their features remain grave, they smile reassuringly back.

Jamie helps me under the covers and sits on the edge of the bed, holding my hand.

"How are you feeling?" Niall asks, to which Sam punches him in the arm. "Ow, what's that for?" Niall whispers harshly, grabbing his arm.

"How do you think she feels, ya idiot?"

"Guys, stop." Finn scowls, then smiles wearily at Jamie and me.

"Not too well, I guess," I relay, smiling, though my head throbs so much it makes my stomach squirm. I can't possibly admit how I really feel—emotionally wrecked, violated, and embarrassed, so *very* much embarrassed.

Niall's frown deepens while Sam grimaces.

Tax, maneuvering through the crowded doorway, enters the room and whimpers as he rests his chin on my leg.

"Hey, boy." I sigh, stroking his soft head. He nuzzles my face with his. "I'm glad to see you, too."

He then walks to the corner of the room and circles twice before lying at the foot of the occupied chair.

My blood runs cold. Anger and despair, in the form of tears, try to bring me down, but I fight them back as I glare at Marcas peacefully sleeping. Clutching my trembling hands around the blanket's edge, I pull it higher, as if I can shield myself from feeling any of it.

"Shae?" Jamie says, squeezing my hand.

Clenching my eyes shut, I try to rid my mind of Marcas and this wretched night. At least long enough to not fall apart when I look back at Jamie and the others.

"Do you remember anything from earlier?" Sam asks again. Apparently, I hadn't heard him the first time.

"Bits and pieces, I guess," I lie again because I don't want to speak of such things. Not here. Not now.

A sharp pain suddenly jabs at my temple, forcing a jarring image of Brad's rage-filled face to flash in my mind. The residual sensation of his forceful grabby hands trailing over my skin sends a shiver of dread through me. Subtly, I shake it off, abhorring the unwanted questions it could bring if Jamie or the others should notice.

"We had a nurse come care of you," Jamie says softly. "She said you hit your head pretty hard. Ya got a nice gouge back there; no stitches, though. But she said for us to keep an eye on you."

"A concussion?" I ask, my body flinching from another unsettling image of Brad popping into my head. I hide it by adjusting my legs under the covers.

"She seems to think so, but not a bad one. Mostly you need rest. She left some pills for the pain. I'll go get you some, okay?" She leaves and returns shortly with a piece of bread, a glass of water, and a large white pill, which I gladly accept.

A nurse. From here? I-I can't have people find out about this! Mom—Dad!

The way Jamie stands there with her shifty, watchful stare, I know she has the answers I need. But how do I get here alone?

The boys watch me, too, guarded and quiet, like I might completely lose it at any moment; they're not entirely wrong.

"Hey, you think you could give us some time?" Jamie asks, facing the guys. "Don't worry, I'll get her tucked snug back in bed," she adds, then gives a warm smile when Niall's brow furrows.

"Sure thing," Finn says, grabbing Jamie's hand and squeezing. "I'll be out here if you need me." Then he lets it fall as he leaves the room.

"Yeah, get some rest, ok, Shae," Niall says, trying to keep his smile wide enough to convince me he's not worried about me. But those pouty eyes fool no one.

"I hope you know we're all here for you," Sam adds, glancing at Marcas, sleeping. Then he gives me an understanding smile and a wink before grabbing Niall's arm and dragging him away as he closes the door behind them.

While Jamie sits beside me on the bed, I peek again at the corner. Marcas' chest moves rhythmically up and down in a slow, steady motion in the shadows, so peaceful, so without concern. It makes my blood burn.

"He's worried about you," Jamie says, watching me.

I huff. "Seems like it."

"It's true. He's been there all night. I tried to get him to sleep on the couch or something, but he wouldn't. He said he needed to be here when you woke up."

Imagining Marcas' face, expressionless and calm, I can't help but recall the bitter resentment evident there only a short while ago. Moments, really. Why would he even care what happened to me, especially if

7

what he had confessed before had indeed been how he felt about me?

"You think he'll hear us?" I whisper even softer.

She shakes her head. "He was too worked up before. I don't think even a train chugging through the room could wake him now." She smiles, but when I don't join in, she adjusts her body on the bed to face me.

I close my eyes. A tear trickles down my cheek. Then another.

Grabbing a tissue from the nightstand, Jamie then wipes my cheeks softly. "Maybe you should rest for a while. We can talk later."

When I open my eyes, she is staring at me. While tears ripple in her eyes, she gives a weary, flat smile.

"No." I sniff. "I'm okay," I say, wiping away another tear that had traveled to my chin.

"Shae, I'm *so* sorry! I can't believe. . ." She blinks back more tears. "I've never been so scared in my life!"

I nod slowly, gripping tightly to the sob lodged in my throat.

"If Marcas hadn't gone out when he did—" she cries in a forced whisper.

A sputtered breath catches in my throat. "If *he* hadn't come out?" I repeat in a bitter whisper. "If it wasn't for him, I'd have never been out there."

"I know, but—"

"I can't believe this!" I gasp, my breaths becoming harder and harder to take. "You're siding with him?"

Her eyes widen, glistening with tears. "No-I—"

"He blamed me for Jared leaving! Did you know that? That I must have been so awful and desperate that I drove him away!"

Shaking her head profusely, she gently puts her hand on my arm. "Shae, he couldn't have known. He'd have never said it—"

"You can't possibly know that." I scowl, jerking my arm free, my hand balled in a fist.

"Shae, please try to stay calm," she says, glancing at Marcas, still asleep. "I don't want you hurting yourself. The nurse said for you to take it easy."

Before I can respond, a loud, rapid triple knock comes at the door. As it slowly opens, I quickly wipe the tears from my cheeks.

Sam peeks his head into the room. "Sorry ladies, but I need Marcas, and it can't wait."

We turn to see Marcas standing, stretching his back, then running his fingers through his messy hair. He looks drowsily at Sam, Jamie, and then me.

I turn away, embarrassment rushing me, leaving a chill of panic behind. Had Marcas heard us talking?

"Thanks, Sam, I'll be out in a sec," Marcas says, slowly walking over to the other side of the bed, over to me.

"Fine, but we kind of need to act fast on this," Sam

9

adds, then leaves the door open ajar as he goes.

When Marcas stops in front of me, my body stiffens.

He clears his throat.

"Shae, please—can we talk?"

I stare at my hands, then the floor, basically anywhere but at him. I can't have his green eyes looking at me full of pity. Nor am I anywhere near ready to talk.

Just go. . .

He shifts his feet. "I have to take care of something important, but I'll be back soon. Then maybe we can?"

His constricted, shaky voice startles me and makes me unsure what to do.

After a moment, I nod twice. It hurts me, but I don't care. I just want him to leave.

Tax stretches, then follows Marcas out of the room.

As soon as the door closes, Jamie grabs my arm. "Shae, you have to give him a chance!"

I continue to stare at the ground.

"Shae, please! He's wrecked. I'm sure he never meant to hurt you like that."

"You weren't there!" I say, looking at her hard through tears. "Marcas made it *very* clear how he feels about me—that he wants nothing to do with me. I've never seen such hatred. Eyes so—" My indignation

10

dissolves into despair. "—cold and cruel, staring back at me." Putting my face in my hands, I sob quietly.

"Don't say that," she says, softly rubbing my shoulder and back. "I know that can't be true."

"Why even be upset over me?" I mumble, sounding muffled and nasally. "Was it out of guilt?" I sniff a sob away. "To make himself feel better for all that's happened? Either way, I *don't* need him!"

"Maybe he realized how much he cares for you and panicked. Maybe that's why he was an idiot!"

"Doubt it." I let out a sardonic snort. "Even if, would you be okay with being treated like that?"

"I wouldn't—"

"Don't even. You would rip him a new one."

"Why won't you just give him the benefit of the doubt?" she says, a little irritated.

I look at her sharply and regret it the second my head is bombarded with pain, but I'm too astonished by her comment to care. "And why won't you just take my side with this?"

Her eyes shadow over with pain. "I do, Shae. Can't you see that? What do you want me to do? Hit him again?"

I gawk at her through my tears.

"I know, can you believe it? Lota good it did, though." She frowns, holding up her hand. "I broke a nail."

The pitiful expression on her face makes me grin a

11

little. Noticing, Jamie does too, but it's not strong enough to last.

"Even with his stupidity, I know he cares about you."

"How can you even believe that?" I say, wiping tears from under my eyes, my smile gone.

"Shae, I just do, ok. He's not all bad. I can feel it."

"Yeah, like we knew Jared wasn't all bad." I snarl.

She cringes, then bites her nail and sits silently for a moment.

"I'm sorry," she finally says, sadness sinking in deep. "I wasn't smart enough to see it. And you got hurt."

"Jamie, that's not what—I only mean, some things can't be seen, especially when we're in the middle of it."

"Like you and that guy?" Her brow creases. "Shae, who was he? What happened?"

Swallowing hard, I tug at my earlobe. The trauma is too real, too raw, to talk about. But I have no choice. Not if I want to stop the nightmares from grabbing hold and never letting go.

"His name's Brad," I say, gulping down the stifling lump of discomfort forming in my throat. "We met a few nights back at Duke's. Things didn't go well then either. Guess he decided to bring backup this time," I say with a mocking smile, as if the ache of it all will somehow cease to exist. Breathing, I hold onto the sob

12

in my throat. "He . . . pinned my arms. I-I couldn't get away." Large tears drip down my cheeks, but I ignore them. "He forced me against the wall," I whisper, my chin quivering.

Jamie gasps, her hand over her mouth. "Did he—"

"No," I say quietly. "He got a knee to the groin instead, which didn't make him too happy."

Her wide eyes narrow and shift to the bruise on my cheek. "No wonder Marcas threw him across the parking lot."

He did? But how did he even know I was in trouble? Was he coming to apologize?

"Man, he was so mad I thought he was going to kill that guy! Sam and Finn had to hold Marcas back." Jamie huffs as if something is funny. "And, if I had known what he'd tried to do to you, I would have gladly let Marcas at him!"

Again, why would Marcas bother to do anything for me? Doesn't he hate me?

"Shae, I didn't even know you'd left. All I saw was Niall and Marcas arguing, and then Niall pushed him. I thought he would get it for sure."

I give a pressed frown. "Poor Niall," I mumble sorrowfully. But still, I can't help but feel pride for the kid. Standing up to Marcas takes guts I didn't think he had in him. Suicidal but still brave.

"Then, when Marcas bolted for the back door, we all ran after him. Shae, there was so much blood!" she says, her voice trembling slightly. "Niall was amazing, though. Scared to death like me but did his best to stop the bleeding. I helped, too; kept your head still." She then lets out a shaky sob. "Shae, I thought you were dead!"

Tears, so many more, fall down our cheeks.

Jamie sniffs and wipes a puddle of tears from under her eyes. "Marcas, he—his hands were shaking. He kept mumbling under his breath like he was arguing with himself. Literally freaked out, wouldn't let anyone near you, like you would break or something. I've never seen him like that before! I had to force him to move back so the nurse could take care of you. And when Finn helped Marcas lay you in the backseat of my car—Shae, I swear I heard Marcas crying!"

My heart pounds in my chest. Cry? Over me? Why?

"He wouldn't leave your side—held your hand, said 'everything was going to be ok,' no wait, different, he said *'different'.*"

"Different, how?" I exhale, examining my hands, wondering which one he'd held and what it would feel like. But should it even matter?

"Something about trying to keep his distance, for your sake. But he never said why, only that he didn't have to anymore."

Looking at Marcas' once-occupied chair, I fight

14

against the powerful desire to believe Jamie, to hold on to the hope that all of this had simply been a colossal misunderstanding.

"Shae, he said he couldn't stop thinking about you from the moment you met. But how? He didn't even say anything, remember—at Duke's, with that girl?"

How could I forget? She practically threw herself at him.

Is that how I had appeared too?

'Please don't leave me . . . I can't live without you!' echoes in my mind. Were they Marcas' words, I'd heard, meant as a ploy or something else entirely?

"That's why you've been siding with him," I say poignantly. "Isn't it? Hearing all that stuff?"

"Maybe I had some inside intel, so what? Doesn't change the fact that I heard it when he didn't think anyone was listening! Come on, Shae, he is thinking about *you!* This is huge!"

I know it is, but I can't let myself believe it. Not now, not without knowing why he said those horrible things to begin with. It just doesn't add up.

"Jamie, I get that you want him to be *that* guy for me, but I can't—he—too many times—so many chances he had to be—I—"

"Shae." Her eyes narrow in on me. "Speak English, please!"

"I didn't—things were fine before," I say, gulping back tears as I recall all Marcas had said and all that

15

had happened leading up to it. I don't want to speak of them; to do so would mean exposing them for the lies they very well could be.

"We talked, laughed. Not once did I force Marcas to hang out with me. He could've left me alone. But no, he kept bumping into me, talking to me, getting to know me, and saying sweet things to make me believe he liked me!

'I don't know. Maybe I was too eager—clingy. Or I saw what I wanted to see happening between us—forcing things like he said."

"No! Not even. It's obvious Marcas sought you out; I don't care what he tried to convince you of. To deny what happened between you—there has to be a reason."

Could Jamie be right? My stomach swirls at the idea, and I scold myself for feeling it.

"Yeah, but then also, things weren't always that good," I say, eyeing her. "He has a darker side. One I'm not sure I can trust."

"Ok, but don't we all sometimes? Don't write him off yet. Let him explain. Guys like that don't confess stuff like that unless there's truth behind it. I don't care that you couldn't hear him say it. Doesn't make it any less true."

"But it's more than just that, Jamie. One minute he's rude and annoyingly arrogant, then suddenly, he's this kind and caring guy, only to have something set him off again, and then he's back to acting the jerk. So many times."

Psychotic, isn't it? To find someone attractive and somewhat appealing who also makes you so irate that you see red.

"Why haven't you told me this?"

"What would I have said? *'Hey, Jamie, your boyfriend's got a jerk for a brother. Stop making me hang out with him!'* No, because you would have accused me of secretly liking him and tried even harder to set us up."

"I would not!" She scoffs. "If I had known, I would have—"

I stare at her knowingly; my eyebrow peaked.

"Fine, I probably wouldn't have listened, but I am now. And don't keep things like that from me. Like ever! I need to know!"

"Sorry," I say, frowning, knowing I should have told her long before now, but speaking of it would have given it a voice—a reality—something I wasn't ready to face.

"I can't believe Marcas acted like that and said those horrible things."

"I know," I say, reaching for the pendant against my chest. Touching bare skin, I gasp.

"No-no, no, no, no, no!" I stammer, scattering the pillows, blankets, and sheets to the side. Dang it! It's not here! How could I have not noticed it missing?

17

My stomach lurches. "Oh no." I gulp hard, realizing the only place left it could be.

"Shae," Jamie says, holding out her hand. "Are you looking for this?"

Seeing the shimmery silver chain, I wail, "Yes!" and grab it as I hug her tightly. It's only a necklace, but the reality of losing it devastated me, like losing a loved one forever.

"Here," she says, taking it from me and clasping it around my neck. "It got snagged on your dress when I was changing you. Marcas helped fix it. There." She sighs, watching me closely as she adjusts it, so it hangs evenly. "Good as new."

I smile at her through my tears, then settle back into the mess of a bed. Leaning against the wall, I clutch the pendant in my hand. Jamie watches me with guarded eyes, probably thinking me insane for my outburst. But then she smiles warmly, and I relax.

"So, you and Marcas are thinking about each other. That's interesting, don't you think? Do you believe he cares about you, then? Maybe enough to call it love?"

"Can't, be . . . caa . . . ause." I yawn again. Finding it harder to keep my eyes open, I pull the messy blankets over me and nestle deep into the mound of pillows. "Grown men don't just fall in love with women they hardly know."

"Sometimes they do," she says. "And you can't

18

know for sure how Marcas feels."

"Neither can you," I add matter-of-factly. "I can't risk being made a fool *again*. My heart wouldn't survive it." Then, as I fight back more yawns, the room teeters in dizzy waves, so I turn on my side and curl up in a ball.

Jamie bites her lip and shakes her head. "But still, there has to be a reason for everything."

I squeeze a pillow to my chest, needing something close to comfort me when nothing else seems to.

"For the first time in so long, it felt amazing to let someone in again, to be cared for like that. But when Marcas said those awful things, it ripped it all away. I'm so confused now—don't know if I want to deal with any of it."

"No, Shae, don't say that. You're just tired and overwhelmed." She touches my leg. "Give Marcas a chance to fix this."

Even if I had wanted to, I didn't have time to respond before there came a timid knock at the door.

My body jolts upright, and I instantly regret the sudden movement. The room is spinning. My heart races rapidly in my chest.

The door slowly opens, and Marcas enters.

Jamie stands up slowly and gives me a knowing look. "I'll be back in a bit." When she moves past Marcas, she smiles. "Not too long, okay?"

He gives a slight nod of understanding before the

19

door closes.

Avoiding looking directly at Marcas, I sit up straighter and turn to the side, letting my legs hang off the side of the bed.

He stops before me, his usually confident stance now slouched and broken.

"Can I sit?" he asks, his voice just as shaky as the rest of him.

I nod.

Ever so gently, he sits beside me. After a long moment, he reaches for my hand. I almost pull away, afraid to be touched and feel his warmth, but I let him take it at the last moment. I don't know why I do, but something inside makes me.

His soft, warm hands feel as unsteady as mine. I can sense his eyes on me. Not wanting to see their gorgeousness looking back at me, I focus on my feet instead, peeking out from under the bedding.

"How's your head?" he asks quietly.

"Bearable, now," I whisper. "What about you? You seemed pretty out of it before."

"I kind of was until the knock woke me." As he tenderly places a strand of my hair behind my ear, he gently turns my face towards him and caresses the bruise on my cheek. "Does it hurt?"

I breathe deeply. His touch is so tender and trusting, I lose my thoughts. "Not really," I finally say, letting the words out slowly.

He looks at our interlocked hands and pauses. When he speaks again, his words quiver. "I only have a minute, but there's so much to say."

I lick my trembling lips. "Tell me why, Marcas." A tear streams down my cheek. Wiping it off, I watch him.

He tilts his head at me, our eyes finally meeting. "I'm so sorry." His voice falters, so he clears his throat and tries again. "For those terrible things I said. For the way I acted."

"I want to know why," I say again, squeezing his hand.

Two tears stream down his cheeks when he blinks his glossy, vibrant green eyes. He quickly wipes them away and sniffs. "I want to explain; believe me, but there's too much to tell you. We need more time than what we have right now."

"I don't know, Marcas—"

He squeezes my hand, clutching it in desperation to his chest. "I'd take it all back if—" He stops again, his words lodging in his throat, utter sorrow in his eyes. "I didn't mean for any of this to happen."

"But it did, Marcas, partly because of what you did. What you said."

"I know, Shae, I—" He sucks in a stutter. "I promise I will never hurt you like that again. I hated how you looked at me because of something I had done. I hurt you, and it kills me."

21

His proclamation, raw and unfiltered like it is, sounds so genuine and honest that it makes my body quake.

When he said my name, I wanted to hug him, pull him close, and forget everything. But I can't. I need to know why this has happened.

"You have every right not to trust me, but when we talk later and I have a chance to explain, you'll see everything for what it is, I promise." His eyes plead with me to say I'll give him a chance, but I don't know if I can give him what he wants.

I clear my throat, but it's too dry. "I hope so." Then, feeling the magnitude of the day, I rest my head on his shoulder.

For a few more minutes, we sit in silence.

As sleep starts to drag me down further, I close my eyes. Then, as if sensing me fading, Marcas squeezes my hand affectionately and says, "Come on, let's get you back in bed."

After helping my legs under the covers, he pulls the blankets up to my chin, then leans in and kisses my forehead. "Get some rest, and I'll see you soon."

Incapable of keeping my eyes open any longer, I only see the hazy outline of Marcas at the door. As he walks out of the room and shuts the door behind him, I finally give in to the sandman and let him take me away.

CHAPTER 2

Different

Several charcoal sketches dot the living room rug. Part of each drawing is highlighted with colored chalk.

The one on the floor next to me is of Jamie and Finn on the couch, asleep in each other's arms, her head resting on his chest, their fingers interwoven. Another sketch, next to the small bookshelf on one side of the couch, is of Sam, his mouth open in laughter and his smiling eyes big and intensely blue. And the one of Niall, resting halfway under the end table, is a rendering of a tall, muscular man with strength in stature and maturity—the man I know that hides deep inside him rather than his current self,

23

who, as we all know, has yet to reach peak potential.

Several pieces of crumpled paper stick out from between the couch cushions.

I am on my fifth attempt at capturing Marcas, but neither his eyes nor lips come out quite right. Fixated on their disproportions, I blow a puff of air at a strand of hair tickling my forehead, and then I begin to aggressively erase all of it.

Tax, asleep at my feet, snorts and jerks his body as he moves his legs in mid-pursuit of some invisible threat.

I smile. "Such a good boy."

While examining the drawing again, I let my fingers caress the pendant against my chest. The habit has a soothing effect on my countenance. I do not know why I feel connected to it, but I do. It is mine now, and I don't want to lose it ever again.

It's been almost a week since I was attacked, and my mind has finally met its match. Boredom—in the most epic of proportions—has destroyed my sanity, leaving days on end with nothing to do but dwell on the past, the muddied present, and, of course, the unknown future.

The morning after, Jamie had taken the nurse's orders for rest to the umpteenth degree, insisting I stay in bed for the foreseeable future. I tried to resist, having woken up feeling much better, but she wouldn't budge.

24

"No one gets better from a head injury that fast!" she had said, quite forcefully, I might add, as she practically strapped me back down.

Not being able to take the confinement any longer, I had tried to convince Jamie that muscle atrophy was a real danger. She refused to listen to reason, fearing that if I were to walk about the house, I'd somehow fall and bust my head open, dying in the process.

She stayed over several days and nights to be sure I followed orders.

One evening, she and Finn tried to make it fun by making dinner: homemade chicken and Alfredo pizza on French bread. It wasn't half bad.

That's when she finally let me out. The couch had never felt so liberating. Sam and Niall were there too, watching their rival baseball game on the new 52-inch television they insisted on buying me—no payback necessary.

"I can't even read the bottom of the screen! Where'd you get that thing, an antique store?" Sam had said.

They should have saved their money because not even a third of the way through, Jamie kicked them out for fighting. They had to finish watching it from the porch window. Sam's tantrum when his team lost made us all laugh, even Jamie.

Eventually, I grew desperate enough for freedom

that I threatened to let it slip to Finn of a time when Jamie had peed her pants at school from laughing too hard. And I wasn't referring to an elementary school accident, either. After that, Jamie miraculously concluded, grudgingly, that I was free to come and go at will.

Even with my independence, I haven't stepped outside much. Jamie thinks I have anxiety, maybe even a bit of PTSD from what happened to me, and that I should probably talk to someone. She may be right; when we sat on the porch yesterday and talked through it some more, it seemed to help.

I don't know how Marcas and the others pulled it off, but no one, not even my parents, had found out about that night. Which, of course, was a relief and a curse all the same. My mother called several times to invite me to dinner. The last time, I almost let it slip why I couldn't make it.

About the only thing my house arrest has given me is ample time to think, ponder, overanalyze, and probably fret a bit too much about Marcas. Mostly, I try to decipher his past and present actions compared to what Jamie told me about him and what I experienced with him when we were alone later that night.

Jamie insisted he'd come to see me since then, but always when I was sleeping. And now that I am back to my old self, I have yet to see him. I secretly wish for it.

The remorse I saw in him was real, tangible. That much, I do know. And yet, even with the void of unanswered questions looming over me, I find that the more time passes, the more things don't seem as dire as I once thought. My heart seems to be beating faster lately, and I wholeheartedly blame Marcas.

Knowing we will eventually talk about everything, I wait and hope he will come find me soon.

Crumpling up my latest attempt at Marcas' face, I toss the wadded paper across the room to the wastebasket. It misses by a long shot, rolling behind the open front door. Sighing forcefully, I retrieve it, then toss it in the garbage.

Tax perks up as my hand touches the handle on the front door. "No, boy, not this time. You'll have to stay put."

His ears fall. Standing, he then slowly walks to me and sniffs around my ankles before going into the kitchen and out the dog door in the back. His collar jingles as he moves.

As I step outside onto the porch, I pull the locked door closed behind me.

The clouds overhead, bulky and billowy white, drift across the sky at a typical steady Montana pace. Walking along the cobblestone path outside the yard, I pass trees in full bloom, with little pink and white flowers covering every branch. Standing next to one, I

27

close my eyes and take deep breaths, inhaling the sweet smell while the warm sun dances across my face.

When I open my eyes, I notice Marcas standing a few feet away, leaning against a large tree. The sun shimmers off his tousled, black hair; his eyes crinkle as he smiles.

As excitement rushes through me, I try to steady my heartbeat as I stroll toward him.

"I thought I might see you out today," he says, smiling wide, pulling me into a warm, gentle hug.

"You did?" I muse, my cheeks reddening as I nestle into his arms, breathing in deep the scent of sandalwood and pine. It comforts me, like home.

He looks at me and strokes his thumb where the yellowish-green bruise had been present as if to rub off any remanence. "You look healthier; cheeks are nice and rosy again." Slowly, his eyes shift to mine.

Eagerness flutters around inside me. Does he feel it too?

For a moment, we are silent.

When he finally releases me, he reaches for the low branch over our heads and hangs on it. "You're outside—that must mean your jailor finally set you free?" He smirks, as if me being locked up like Rapunzel is funny.

"Shhh, you want to get me in trouble or something?" I laugh.

28

Marcas leans in. "Your laugh—I've missed hearing it." A sexy grin crosses his lips, making me lightheaded.

Picking a budding blossom from a branch by his arm, I press it to my nose and inhale its fragrance as I trail off in thought.

"Is everything okay?" he asks with a hint of concern.

I smile and take a long breath. "Just thinking about stuff, I guess. A lot's happened lately."

"You mean since you met me?" he says somberly.

I shrug and grin.

"I promised you a talk, didn't I?"

"Why haven't you come to see me?"

He glances away.

I hold my breath, suddenly worried that I may not like the answer he gives.

He looks at me, a hint of sadness in his eyes. "Honestly? I wasn't sure you wanted me to."

"Marcas—"

"I know you said to, and I didn't mean to keep you waiting, but I figured you needed more time. Then I got nervous that you might have changed your mind."

My heart sputters wildly. N*ervous about me?*

"But I also went out of town for a few days."

I grin. "Work?"

"Always is," he says with a crooked smile.

A refreshing, delicate breeze rustles the branches

29

above us as I twirl the flower between my fingers like a parasol. "I love these—always have," I say as I smell them.

"There's so many; very beautiful," he adds, staring into my eyes as if he really meant it about me.

"My parents have them in their front yard, too," I continue, ignoring how his look makes my heart patter. "As a kid, I made crowns with them and wore them everywhere, pretending for hours to be the queen of the forest." I laugh lightheartedly. "The smell still takes me back." Then I gaze up into the blossoming branches toward the warm sun. It feels so lovely.

"Ever have a smell bring memories back like that?" I ask, looking at him and holding the flower out for him to take.

"Sometimes," he says, taking it from me and with it my hand. "But I don't like to dwell on the past."

As he places the flower behind my ear, a sudden gust of wind swirls blossoms down from the tops of the trees, falling like delicate snowflakes all around us. The sunlight shines through the branches, dispersing bright rays across the ground.

Marcas takes strands of my hair between his fingers and rubs them together softly. "Hmm, I've never noticed that before. They shine like fire in the sun. So beautiful." Letting them fall, he looks into my eyes. "Have you given any more thought about me?"

My stomach flips. "Quite a bit, actually," I muse.

"I was hoping you would say that." He smirks. "But first, I might have something else that might interest you."

"Oh really?" I grin happily.

"How does a rodeo with Jamie and Finn sound? We could all have dinner afterward. Then maybe you and I could go talk."

"I'd like that," I say, suppressing the excitement I feel as I picture Marcas holding my hand for the rest of the day.

"Excellent!" His hidden dimples appear on his cheeks, making my pulse flutter spastically like a hummingbird.

For a moment, we stare into each other's eyes.

Then, Marcas leans in slowly, making my body quiver with expectation. Sliding his hand up the back of my neck, he pulls me closer, his lips an inch away from mine.

The desire to kiss him rushes over me like a warm fire.

Just do it—kiss me!

When his soft lips touch mine, every nerve in my body bursts to life; the more they come, the more they consume me.

Eventually, he pulls back and rests his forehead against mine. Breathing in deep, as if taking in everything, from my scent to the electrifying power surging between us that I know we both can feel, he smiles a sheepish grin. "I probably shouldn't have done that." His voice holds a hint of remorse.

I can't keep the corny, rosy-cheeked smile from stretching across my face. "No, probably not."

His dimples return when an impish smirk appears on his face as he steps back. "Come on, let's take a walk." Then he squeezes my hand, still in his.

"To where?"

"Jamie's shop. Finn's probably hanging around there somewhere."

I step toward him, expecting us to keep moving, but he doesn't. Instead, he leans down and gently kisses my forehead. "I'm glad you're feeling better, Shae," he adds, peering deeply into my eyes.

A tingle travels from his kiss down through my body like a surge of energy. At the same time, I feel the pendant around my neck radiate warmth against my skin like flames from a warm campfire on a chilly night, hot yet comforting. I'm beginning to see a pattern with it, but then again, how can I be sure—my whole body is burning with eagerness.

With my hand in his, we walk down the path into town. When we pass the two large windows of the flower shop, bells above the door ding, and the customer stepping out holds the door for us to enter. The wonderfully overwhelming, sweet aroma of fresh flowers fills my nose.

32

Finn is leaning against the counter, watching Jamie shuffling back and forth from the glass case to the counter, combining papers with their designated flower arrangements as she moves.

"Working hard, I see!" I call loudly.

"Shae!" Jamie squeals and rushes over.

Marcas joins Finn at the counter while Jamie wraps her arms around me and squeezes the life out of me.

Letting me go, she spots the flower in my hair and plucks it out, eying it suspiciously. "What have you two been up to?"

I shrug while suppressing the grin that desperately wants to shine for all to see.

"Alright, don't tell me." She eyes me skeptically. "But does this mean you're coming, because I warned—"

"Jamie." I laugh. "Yes,"

"Yes!" she hisses, gripping my arm tightly. "Me and Finn—you and Marcas!"

Her enthusiasm is intoxicating, threatening to pollute me entirely, but that can't happen—not in public, not with Marcas within earshot. No one needs to witness such girlish hysterics.

"So, I was thinking maybe we could. . ." she jabbers on, her voice fading as I watch Marcas. He is watching me, too, and smiles. This time, I don't shy away, happy to have his attention.

33

With every genuinely purposeful moment we have, the more the questions I hold on to dissolve away. I know I shouldn't let them, but Marcas has changed—no longer consumed with hiding who he is and what he wants.

"Enough already," Jamie huffs, pulling on my arm. "You have all night with him; concentrate, please!"

"Sorry." I beam back at her as waves of giddiness course through my veins.

"You really like him, don't you?"

"Jamie, please."

"You do! I can see it in that huge, cheesy smile plastered on your face!"

She tries to poke my cheeks, but when I veer to the side to escape it, my leg hits a metal bucket of flowers, spilling water on the floor. The loud bong of the wobbling container echoes, making us giggle.

The shop door abruptly opens, and a gentleman with thinning hair and bottle-rimmed glasses comes in and heads straight for us.

While Jamie works, I mop up the spill before going over to the guys.

They stop talking.

Eyeing them narrowly, I ask, "What are you two talking about?"

Marcas slips his arm around my waist, drawing me to his side with ease. "You two figure it all out?" he asks, grinning.

34

"I don't care what we all do as long as my woman is with me, and we get to see some bull ridin'!" Finn says with a thick cowboy twang as he puts something in his wallet.

"Good to know." I laugh while Marcas rolls his eyes. "I think Jamie's almost done; then we can get outa here."

"Actually, you think we could meet in about a half hour?" Finn asks, giving Marcas a quick glance. "There's something I need to do really quick."

"Sure." I shrug. "Jamie's place, then? I'm sure she'll want to change."

Marcas leans down and kisses my cheek. "Be there soon."

They leave, and I peruse the flower arrangements scattered about the room while I wait for Jamie.

Finally, she finishes, and the customer leaves.

While grabbing her purse, Jamie calls to the back room, "Bye, I'll see you Monday!" A "Have fun." returns to her.

With arms interlocked, Jamie and I leave out the front door. Before turning the corner of the building, she hands me an unmarked, white envelope, the flap tucked in. I eye her dubiously as I open it and pull out a slip of paper.

When my eyes widen, she smiles. "My commission from that wedding. Pretty cool, huh?"

"Five hundred dollars?" I scoff. "Don't you owe

35

me this exact amount?" I tease, fanning my face with the check.

She laughs.

"Shopping spree?" I ask. Knowing her, it's already spent.

"Actually—something for Finn," she says, looking at me hesitantly.

I eyeball her with mocking shock.

"Seriously!" She scoffs, giving a look an unamused mother would give as she grabs the envelope and paper from my hands. "I mean it; what do you think?"

"Honestly? It's kind of big."

"Good! I want him to know how much I care."

"And you're sure he feels the same?" I nudge her shoulder, teasing again.

"He better, or I'm wasting my time."

"He does, trust me!"

While walking past the bookstore, we both wave at Lainey through the front window, and she waves back.

"You know, sometimes I panic, thinking he'll see how self-involved I am and dump me," Jamie continues.

"Don't be ridiculous."

"No, I'm serious. We both know how I can be."

Unwilling to confirm nor deny such a statement, I laugh. But it hardly matters. I've seen the way he looks at her. Talk about worshiping the ground she walks on. In those love-struck eyes of his, she can do no wrong.

"But that's not what this is about, is it?" I counter with a grin. "You really like him, and you're scared."

"You're damn right I am! Scared he'll see right through me. That he'll find someone better. Or get bored and leave!"

"I wouldn't worry so much," I say as we walk up to her apartment building and stop.

"How can I not? This is real for me. I can't screw it up!" Her eyes mirror a familiar melancholy I know so well.

"Jamie, the poor guy's head over heels. Besides, think how great it all is; way worth it."

Jamie punches the code on the keypad to the left of the door and waits for the beep. The door kicks open, and we step into the lobby.

"I'm surprised you think that, especially after what's happened," she says as we take a left and head down a small hallway before stopping in front of apartment 9A.

Jamie pulls keys from her bag, inserts one into the lock, and then pauses, "You scared about Marcas?"

"Constantly," I sigh, resting my back against the wall.

"You can't hide anymore, Shae." Jamie moves away from the door, leaving the keys still in the lock, and leans against the wall beside me. She rests her head on my shoulder as we stare across the hall at a picture of a prickly, out-of-focus potted cactus.

"Sure, Jared broke your trust—your heart—but don't let him dictate the rest of your life. Don't give him the power to ruin something really great! You deserve happiness—love, comfort, support, and trust. All that and so much more! None of which he gave you, by the way. If anything, he did you a huge favor by leaving."

Her words hang heavy in my mind. Having never thought of it that way, I almost cry. I have let regret and pain stop me from living and from seeing the real blessing in all this. I am free! Free to find real love—lasting love—something I never truly believed I could have for myself.

"Marcas isn't anything like Jared. You get that, right?" she coos.

"I'm very aware." I smile, patting atop her head.

She moves back to the door and opens it. It slams shut behind us as we go inside her apartment.

"How are things with Marcas?" she asks, tossing keys in a glass bowl on a table by the door, then kicks her shoes off into the box at the end of the couch.

Biting my lip, I shrug. "Good, I guess. I mean, I want to believe it when he says things are different now. But a part of me feels like it could revert to how it was."

"That'll never happen," Jamie says with an

38

assurance I doubt she can verify.

Unsure if I should believe as she does, I shrug. "Maybe." Then I sit on the loveseat. "It's probably best if I take it slow—just to be safe." I smile.

"Yeah, but not too slow," she warns sharply. "I don't know how you do it—willpower of a nun or something to resist that sweet body of his for so long?" Her lips spread into a wide grin.

I roll my eyes and threaten to chuck a pillow at her from the couch when she walks past to the bedroom.

While she gets ready, I move to the bathroom, checking myself in the mirror. The light denim capris I'm wearing rest perfectly on my hips, while the silky, light-pink blouse with shimmery white buttons accentuating my waist and chest makes me feel more like myself for the first time in a very long time. The only problem lies when I see my face staring back at me: pale cheeks, unmagnified eyes, undefined lips.

"Makeup in the mirror if you need any," Jamie calls from the bedroom as if she read my mind. "But watch out. The door sticks and stuff falls out. I lost my favorite lipstick in the stupid toilet the other day," she grumbles.

Lucky for me, it's already open.

With a puffy brush, I dab a little blush on my cheeks, then add a coat of black mascara, making the hazel in my eyes pop. Deciding to leave my hair down,

I part it on the side and tuck it behind my ears, the ends curling upward.

Leaning close to the mirror, I examine a few strands of hair to see the shimmer Marcas talked about before. But, finding only brown in the dim light of the room, I give up.

A few minutes later, Jamie joins me dressed like a model, wearing a tight, white cap-sleeved shirt, dark skinny jeans, a worn pair of cowboy boots, and a tan cowboy hat on her head. Her hair, wavy, blonde, and voluptuous, hangs loosely down her back.

I frown.

"What?" she asks with a quick look in the mirror. Seeing nothing wrong, she looks at me, perplexed. I reply with a tug at my clothes.

"Oh, bother, Shae; you look great. Believe me, it's a drastic improvement." She smiles as she runs her fingers through her hair. "I should probably thank Marcas for that," she adds, then bumps her hip with mine, setting me off balance.

I stumble over my own feet and catch myself on the doorframe. "Oh gee, thanks."

"You guys talk yet?" she asks, ignoring my frowning face.

With a shrug of my shoulder, I sigh and lean against the doorframe.

"Seriously?" she says while dabbing brown eyeshadow on her lids.

40

"He said he didn't know if I wanted him to come over."

"Uh yeah, you told him to."

"I know!"

"So, if you didn't talk." She lifts her brow. "Then what did you do?"

"Not what you're implying, thank you."

"Come on, spill. A sista needs to know."

"Like I said, we're taking things slow."

She tilts her head to the side, her eyes burrowing skepticism into me. The interrogation becomes a staring contest, which I never win, my eyes drying out too fast to give me a fighting chance. So, this time, I concede early.

"Fine." I huff, blinking rapidly, my eyes watering. "We kissed, ok. You happy now?" I add, folding my arms.

"I knew it!" she states matter-of-factly, then puckers her plump lips to add ruby-red lip gloss before rubbing them together. "Come on, don't leave me hangin'; how was it? Fireworks? Spasms all over your body? What?"

My cheeks turn as red as her lip gloss, and when I don't answer, her eyes narrow as she places her hand on her hip, head cocked to the side.

"Ugh, all right," I say, letting a smirk finally appear on my face. "It was amazing. Incredible even. *So* much more than expected."

Reliving the kiss again in my mind sends twinges of joy fluttering through my body. Even now, I can still feel the pressure of his lips on mine.

Jamie's cheeks puff up in a large grin.

"So, help me, Jamie, don't you dare say anything to Finn about this!"

She shushes the idea away with a feeble wave, like it's utterly preposterous and so not something she would do. But I know her; oh, how I do.

Walking back to the living room, I add, "I mean it, Jamie, not a word."

She doesn't respond.

Two seconds later, a knock sounds at the front door.

"Can you grab that? I'm almost ready," she says, darting back across the hall to the bedroom.

Waves of nervousness wiggle inside my chest as I open the door. Finn stands front and center, a massive smile on his face. Sticking to the country theme, he wears a striped navy-blue button-down shirt, light blue jeans, and a black cowboy hat, looking perfect for a night among cowboys.

"Hey—whoa, you look great!" I say, letting him through. Jamie waits in the middle of the room, where he hands her a long-stem, red rose from behind his back.

I turn back to the door. Marcas is standing in the hall, a sexy smile on his lips. His dark jeans and baby

42

blue button-down shirt, with the sleeves rolled up just enough to show off muscular forearms and accentuate his biceps, makes my knees weak.

A lock of hair hangs down over his forehead, and as he runs his fingers through it, pushing it back into place, he smiles even brighter at me. His other hand holds a small bundle of my favorite flowers.

With a tug of my wrist, he pulls me into the empty hall and draws me close as he rests his hands on my waist. "Are you as excited for this as I am?" he whispers, his eyes twinkling as he gazes into mine.

You have no idea!

I nod and smile as I try to steady my breathing. But knowing how much he wants this too is almost more than my spastic heart can take.

He breathes deeply. "You look incredible today, by the way."

Unable to stop my cheeks from burning red, I look away. With a gentle touch of his fingers on my chin, Marcas tilts my face to meet his, a sweet smile lighting up his face.

Consumed by the desire to kiss him, I move in close. When our lips meet for the second time today, I feel sparks explode in every cell of my body, making my head spin and forcing away any other thought but him.

Finn clears his throat, interrupting our moment like an earth-shattering boom, which earns him a solid smack on the back from Jamie.

As I smile sheepishly and lay my head against Marcas' chest, his heart beating fast in my ear, Marcas hands me the small bouquet of flowers. Their familiar scent makes me smile more. At this moment, I feel like the queen I once pretended to be.

Jamie locks the door, then she and Finn walk past us and down the hall.

Holding hands, Marcas and I follow close behind them.

CHAPTER 3

A Moment's Peace

Going full speed and nostrils flaring, a brown and white-spotted horse zooms through the arena gates.

Within seconds, the horse reaches one of three fifty-five-gallon metal drums, forming a large triangle in the center of the arena. A large dust cloud billows under its hooves as the horse narrowly rounds the barrel and dashes even faster to the second. Dark wet stains are visible under its belly strap. The graceful creature curves around the final barrel and sprints through the center of the ring to the finish line. The horse skids to a stop as the female rider whirls her white cowboy hat above her head. Fans scattered throughout the bleachers, cheer and whistle with delight.

Over the loudspeaker, two men debate the horse's physical condition and how it will affect the rider's time before analyzing the rider's form and abilities to lead her horse to the finals.

They announce bull riding is next.

Sitting beside me on worn, whitewashed wooden bleachers holding my hand, Marcas watches with wide-eyed wonder as a bull is shimmied into the bucking chute.

"I thought you said you'd been to one of these before," I say.

"A few." He grins and uses the program to block the sun as he looks at me. "But it never gets old. See." He points. "You have these massive beasts pitted against men strapped on their backs. And at that moment, a mere eight seconds can feel like a lifetime, not only for the rider and bull but also the spectators."

While he goes back to watching the rider mount his bull, I wonder just how deep his well of thought goes. He's not like other guys, obsessed with girls and partying all the time, and I'm glad for it. I find his maturity sexy.

Rodeo clowns dressed in patched overalls with polka-dot suspenders, a bright red nose, and a painted white face roll wooden barrels to designated spots on opposite sides of the dirt arena and then climb inside.

Next to us, Jamie and Finn snuggle up close to each other with Jamie's arm around Finn's back.

Jamie leans over and whispers in my ear, "Hey Shae, you hungry?"

I laugh, "It's not even 4 o'clock yet!"

"So, I forgot to eat. Come with me!"

I turn to Marcas. He's so enthralled with what's happening in the arena that I almost hate to disturb him.

"Jamie's hungry," I whisper. "We're going to grab something really quick. You want anything?"

He looks at me and smiles. "Not really." Then he reaches into his back pocket. "But here, let me give you—"

"Me neither." I smile, putting my hand on his arm. "Just tagging along."

Giving a shrug, he puts his wallet back in his pocket. "I guess have fun then," he says with a wink. It's a new gesture from him, and I like how it makes me feel.

Jamie and I walk down the bleachers and out the gate. The concessions are on the opposite side of the fairgrounds, across from the carnival games and rides. The giant Ferris wheel consumes the bright blue, tree-lined skyline, turning clockwise against the forest background. The beeps and plinking sounds of the games grow louder as we move closer to the carnival and up to a food truck with a giant corndog in an apron on the roof. The line to order is at least

47

seven people deep. Nonetheless, it's the shortest line we see.

At the ticket booth across from us, a young boy holds hands with his older brother, waiting to buy tickets. The games' mesmerizing pull and magical allure make their faces light up with excitement, like on Christmas.

Suddenly, the familiarity of everything around us forms a heavy sensation that settles in my stomach.

"Hey, you remember that pushy guy from your shop?" I ask Jamie as we step forward in line. "The one on the fourth?"

"Geeze, that was ages ago," Jamie responds promptly. "What brought him up?"

"All this," I say, looking around. "Did he ever come back, you think?"

She shakes her head and shrugs. "Unless Marge forgot to tell me."

I nod. "Right." And I try to forget it. But I can't shake the feeling of unease floating thick in the air.

"You know, I wouldn't be surprised if that Brad guy sent him," Jamie says plainly as if it were as blasé as a passing thought. But it is anything but simple for me.

Seeing my face go white, she frowns. "Hey, Shae, that loser's long gone; he can't hurt you now."

As notable knots twist in my stomach, I scrunch my brow. "Yeah, I know." Then I give a slight smile to

48

assure her I am all right, even though I don't think I am.

"Man, I have to pee!" she says, crossing her legs while reaching into her deep pockets. "Do me a favor and order me a. . ." She pauses, pursuing the menu. "Oh, a giant corn dog, a medium diet soda, and a bag of caramel corn." She then shoves a wad of crinkled cash in my hands.

I raise my eyebrows at her.

"What?" she added with a grunt, still digging for more money out of her tight jeans. "I said I was hungry; besides, the corn is for Finn anyway."

After piling the last of her cash in my cupped hands, Jamie rushes to the port-a-potties back at the arena entrance.

As I sift through the bills, straightening them individually, a sudden wind rips one from my clutches, sending it somersaulting across the dirt. Chasing after it, I try to grab it as it drifts and rolls between the legs of people walking by. Just when I am about to lose it in the crowd, a shiny black leather boot stomps down on it, making a cloud of dust rise up around it.

A man chuckles. "Wow there, I got you!" he says, reaching down to take the bill from underfoot.

Blocking the sun with my hand, a tall man comes into view with brunette hair, muscular shoulders, and lips in a crooked smile.

"This, get away from you?" he asks.

Something about his piercing, golden eyes makes me pause. I swallow hard as I straighten up. "Uh yeah, it did, thanks."

At first, he holds the money out for me to take but then teasingly pulls it away when I reach for it.

"Hold on now. Does the pretty have a name?"

"What does it have to do with getting my money back?" I say, narrowing my stare.

"Ah, see, it doesn't." He grins. "But what could it hurt?"

The flicker of mockery in his voice triggers recognition in my mind. But I still can't place where I know him. I watch him more closely.

"It's Shae," I finally huff and stretch my hand out.

"Shae? That's unique—strong—I like it," he muses, putting his hand in mine instead of the money. "I'm Conall." He gives two vigorous shakes before adding a light tug to pull me closer. Then, with his eyes casually searching the crowd, he adds, "You out on an evening like this alone, *Shae*?"

A shot of warning surges down my spine.

"Uh, that is definitely none of your business." I scowl, tugging my hand free from his firm grip and stepping back.

His lips form a teasing smile. "And yet, my curiosity is still piqued."

A man to my right steps out of the crowd and casually moves toward us. Then another on my left.

Breathing hard, I step back, the awful, familiar feeling of entrapment weighing down on me.

"Wait," Conall says with an eerie chuckle. "Don't you want your money?"

"You keep it," I say sharply and rush to the crowd, but a bald-headed gargantuan man blocks my way.

Heavy like lead, my feet skid over the dirt ground to a stop. My body stiffens as I focus on the jagged scar traveling from the top of his eyebrow down to the middle of his cheek.

"Rogan, goodness man, don't go scaring the poor thing," Conall says, walking around his large counterpart, then he stretches out his hand, the dollar crumpled in his palm for me to take.

"Like I said, you keep it." I'm breathing so hard now I feel lightheaded.

"Shae?" I hear Jamie calling as she makes her way through the crowd. Seeing me, she rushes over.

"Hey, there you are. I thought you were getting me—" She gasps, her eyes wide. "You!" Grabbing my arm, she forcefully pulls me behind her. "You get the hell out of here right now!" she growls at Conall. "And tell that piece of crap, Brad, to leave Shae alone!"

Conall narrows his eyes at her.

Brad? My knees quiver as I grip Jamie's arm. My body is so stiff I wouldn't be able to move even if I tried. The man from the shop!

Conall glares at her with cold, hard eyes, yet his malevolent grin returns. "Not friends?" he snarls and

51

steps up to her. "Perhaps I was too soft on you back at that little shop of yours." Then, with lightning speed, he reaches around her, snatches my wrist, and twists it as he whips me forward.

"Hey!" Wincing in pain, I grit my teeth. "What are you—?"

Jamie tugs my arm, fighting against him, but he shoves her back. She falls hard to the ground. When she gets up and dusts herself off, anger is so sharp in her eyes that they could cut steel.

One of the other men tries to grab Jamie's arm, but she pulls free, whips around, and stomps on his foot. "Get your filthy hands off me!" she huffs hard, her body shaking, but her conviction radiating through her scowl. "I mean it; let Shae go!" She steps closer to Conall. "Your craphead boss, Brad, hightailed it out of here over a week ago. Or didn't you get the memo? So, give it up already!"

"Enough!" Conall booms.

Jamie flinches but doesn't back down.

"I don't give a damn who this Brad person is, and I assure you, I work for no one." Annoyed with me still struggling to get free, he shakes my arm violently to make me stop squirming. "As for you," he grunts, squeezing my arm tight. "You're a clever minx—eluding me for so long. Hunting should never be this hard. Entertaining, yes, but irritating just the same. And I grow tired of this game." He spits the words out through clenched teeth close to my face. "It

52

is done. And I have no intention of letting you get away this time!"

"Conall!" Marcas hollers, glaring fiercely as he advances toward us. "Let her go!"

Finn, at his side, mimics a look of contempt.

"Marcas!" I say, my heart leaping.

Conall wrenches my arm even tighter around my back. "Will these incessant interruptions never cease?" he growls while I cry out in pain.

Marcas steps up on Conall. "I said, let her go!" He snarls through clenched teeth as he rips Conall's hand from my arm, flings it away, and then moves me back behind him.

Without hesitation, Jamie runs to the protection of Finn's outstretched arms.

Conall's face holds a subpar, shocked yet knowing look. "Marcas, my boy, so good to see you."

"What do you think you are doing, Conall?" Marcas glares at him. "You're not supposed to be anywhere near here," he adds as he forces us all to take a second cautionary step back.

"On the contrary, Marcas, I belong here just as much as anyone," Conall says smoothly as he rubs his arm where Marcas had gripped it. "As for why I am here." His lips slowly turn up into a smile. "Oh, I'm sure you can guess." Then, with a slight point of his brow, he adds, "But Marcas, seriously, I'm dying to know—how's the hunt going? You find it yet?"

Marcas' scowl deepens. "That's none of your business."

Conall's eyes narrow, burning with anger. "Wrong!" he snaps back.

Startled, I grip Marcas arm even tighter. He doesn't seem to notice.

"After all," Conall says coolly, his tone back to its happy falsehood. "Your business is our business now, isn't it?" His eyes darken slightly. "That is, of course, why we're all here. And look at you, wasting your precious time out frolicking with the locals. What would mother think?" He gives a sardonic batting of his long lashes in mockery as he smirks.

Marcas moves forward, but I won't let go of his arm, gripping it so tight my fingers hurt.

Conall chuckles quietly as he looks at me. "I can tell by your sweetheart's perplexed expression that you haven't told her yet. Tisk, tisk, Marcas, so thoughtless of you. How ever will she take it?"

"Leave her out of this." Marcas snarls, his body tensing even more.

Having seen Marcas this angry once before, I grip his arm with both hands and plant my feet. I won't let him get hurt protecting me.

"Oh Marcas, now you know damn well I can't do that. You made her a part of this when you *took* what was rightfully mine, and I've come to reclaim it."

Claim what? Me? I look sharply around Marcas and see Conall's contorted face of contempt looking back at me. His lips form an evil grin.

"Face it, Marcas, two separate games—with the same outcome," he snickers, his words slithering out like a venomous snake. "And I won't give up on either."

"You will not touch her!" Marcas roars, lunging at Conall out of my tight grasp like it was nothing. Finn quickly grabs Marcas' other arm, stopping him just in time.

"Don't engage Marcas; it's what he wants," Finn says, glaring at Conall.

"That's right, Marcas; listen to the pup for once, and maybe one of you may find yourself still alive after all this is over."

Marcas struggles even harder against Finn, but he won't let Marcas through.

Finn puts a hand on his shoulder. "You have to be strong—think of Shae!"

Panic lodges in my chest. What is going on? Did Conall just say someone would die?

Marcas looks at me. Seeing the worry deep in my eyes, the fury in him subsides. He gives a slight nod, and Finn lets him go.

Reaching for my hand, Marcas holds it tight as he shifts me back behind him again, then faces Conall. "You can try all you want, but you will *never* succeed—at any of it."

55

Conall laughs ironically, "You think you can stop me. I have—" He pauses and gives a knowing grin. "On second thought, I'll save that little surprise for later."

"There won't be a later because I want you out of here, now," Marcas says, with such absolution, that I know he will stop at nothing to make sure Conall leaves for good. And I'm scared he will get hurt trying.

For a moment, Conall hesitates, a shimmer of doubt sparking inside his eyes as if a part of him believes it too.

Marcas takes a single step toward Conall, and Conall's two friends do likewise. Scarface Rogan remains still.

"Tavis, Luc, stay!" Conall barks.

Instinctively, I reach for the necklace around my neck and clasp it tightly in my shaking hand. My movement catches Conall's attention. A sudden ominous shadow drifts over his features as a broad, wicked smile consumes his lips. He then lets out an evil laugh that chills me through.

"Marcas, my boy, you've been holding out on me!" His eyes dance with eager excitement. "It seems I have a serious decision to make regarding your young love. But unfortunately, things don't look good for the two of you, I'm afraid."

Marcas snarls, his teeth clenched. "Don't mess with me, Conall. You will maintain peace. That's an order!"

56

"You're not my king. Neither was your father." Conall's evil grin widens. "He's dead, so I say anything goes."

"Traitor!" Finn barks, and Marcas gives him a look of warning for doing so.

Marcas' hand clamps into a tight fist, but he remains calm and collected. "You may think that Conall, but I assure you, like your father before you, you will fail."

"You're wrong!" Conall bellows in an animalistic roar. "You foolish, lovesick, weakling—I am ten times the man my father was, so don't you dare underestimate what I'm capable of! And if you think we're the only ones drawn here by its presence, you're gravely mistaken. There are others, and a lot more are yet to come. You think you can fight us all? You know damn well she's as good as dead if they get their hands on her." His eyes narrow, and a slight snicker crosses his mouth. "And if one of them should succeed, well then, I guess all I have to do is sit back and wait."

"Enough!" Marcas commands with such a heavy weight that it stills everyone walking around us, who up until now haven't shown the slightest interest in us, which is very odd. "Leave—now!"

Panic rips at my insides. I want to scream, run, or do anything but stay here. Conall said someone was going to kill me! Who? Why?

For a minute, the bystanders watch us. But when nothing happens worth sticking around for, they move on.

Conall stares at Marcas with narrow eyes. Marcas holds his own, his tall, rigid body seemingly towering over Conall.

"As you wish, my lord," Conall finally says, adding a half bow of mockery. Then, with a sly shift of his eyes, he looks at me, the corner of his mouth snarling into an evil grin. I instantly feel sick. Then he and his men turn and leave, going past the rodeo stands and out of sight.

Without hesitation, Marcas draws me to his side and wraps his arm around my shoulder, hurrying us away.

"Marcas, wha-I-I," I stammer as we zig-zag through the crowd.

My body is shaking so much that my legs won't move to the point that Marcas is forced to drag me along.

He stops. "Shae, please listen to me. I know you're scared, but we need to get you out of here. You have to move! Can you do that for me? Can you run?"

His furrowed brow worries me.

Finally, I nod. And before I can even prepare, we are off and running. Marcas is moving so fast that I have to grip his hand tightly just to keep up.

When we finally reach the car, he stops and faces me; his eyes, consumed with worry, still hold a hint of affection as he gives me a quick kiss on my lips. Then he gently removes his arm from my death grip as if my fingers are made of clay and opens the car door for me. Jamie joins me in the back seat.

As I look out the back window at the crowds of people coming and going from the arena, new waves of worry wash over me. That guy could still be in there somewhere, watching my every move. Waiting and planning. For what? I don't even know.

Jamie grips my hand, her eyes just as wide and full of fear as mine. I face forward again as Marcas veers the car from its parking spot and drives on.

Focused on the road, Marcas glances in the rearview mirror at me every so often, his lips pressed together. Soon his face becomes contorted into a troublesome scowl as he drives.

"Marcas," Finn says cautiously. "We have to tell them!"

Marcas shakes his head stiffly. "Not without Sam and Niall."

Silence fills the car, making the thirty-minute drive as agonizing as one might think.

My brain spins widely—so many questions come at me all at once, and I can't answer a single one.

Who is this Conall guy? How does he know Marcas? It's obvious there is some kind of family feud happening—something about Conall's dad trying to do something to Marcas', or something like that. But

59

how could any of that possibly hold a connection to me, let alone a threat to my life?

Eventually, Finn grabs his phone and presses a button as we reach town.

"Hey, you near the cabin?" he pauses, listening to a muffled response. "Don't bother; just get Niall and come on." I hear Sam's heated reply, most likely protesting having to leave some girl he just met. "Dude, give it a rest. We'll be there in five." When Finn hangs up, he glances at Marcas, who doesn't notice or at least doesn't feel the need to acknowledge it.

We drive through town and turn east at the town park before continuing until the road switches to dirt. Eventually, we reach a fork in the path; the left leads to a ghost town about six miles away, but we keep to the right and head in the opposite direction for several more minutes.

We stop in front of a tall gate with barbed wire coiled around the bars. Finn jumps out and opens it, allowing us to drive through before closing it and getting back in.

Marcas keeps a fast pace, moving smoothly and steadily despite the road's uneven surface. Out the window, the trees on the side of the road get thicker and taller the farther into the older part of the forest we travel. I look out the back window to see if anyone is following, but I can only see a cloud of dust kicking up behind us.

A small, rundown wooden house on what looks like stilts creeps into view when we round a corner and drive up a small hill. A wooden staircase leads up to an oversized deck with two large windows overlooking the yard beyond it. Sam and Niall are waiting by the base of the steps.

From the front seat, Finn lifts Jamie's hand and kisses it. "Give us a sec," he says, gazing lovingly at her as the car stops. She nods and smiles wearily.

Marcas turns in his seat. "I'll send Niall when we're ready for you." A smile crosses his lips but doesn't quite reach his eyes. I wish I could get myself to smile back, but I'm too worried to even attempt it. It doesn't matter, though, because he and Finn exit the car and join their brothers at the stairs before I even have a chance to try.

"Jamie, what the hell is going on?" I say the second the door closes, my hands and voice shaking.

"Seriously, I have no idea. I thought—I thought he was Brad's—"

"Me too! But then why threaten me?"

"I—I don't know!"

Growing more agitated, I fidget with the necklace and stare out the window. "That Rogan guy—scar—big!" I say, grasping for coherent thought, but nothing fits together.

Jamie bites her nails and also stares out the window.

61

Marcas and his brothers talk heatedly, pointing into the woods and past the house. Then Marcas, Sam, and Finn walk around the back of the house while Niall comes over to the car and opens the door. He fakes a smile, worry thick in his eyes.

"Hey, Shae. Jamie. The guys want us inside."

"Niall, what's going on?" I say hurriedly.

"I can't tell you."

"Why the hell not?" Jamie counters.

"Shae, try and have an open mind. Marcas did what he thought was best."

My stomach tightens. "Marcas—what's best?" I retort. "I am so sick of hearing that."

Niall reaches out his hand. "Please, Shae, trust me." His soft smile, the one he gives to comfort me, breaks me down; I cannot fight it. Giving a slight nod, I take his hand, and he pulls me out.

Jamie and I follow Niall up the stairs, through the house's entryway, and down a long hall into a small living room and kitchen common room. Light beams through the clean windows, casting branch-shaped shadows on the carpeted floor. An old coo-coo clock ticks loudly, reminding me of one my grandfather used to have.

The air, musty and hot, warms my frigid, worry-filled body as I hesitantly sit on a loveseat tucked back against the two windows facing the yard. Its red, green, and brown plaid cushions with matching armrest covers are faded and worn.

62

"You live here?" Jamie asks, eyeing her surroundings. "It's so . . . old." Then she plops down on the armchair beside me, kicking up a dust cloud into the sunlight, looking like microscopic pieces of glitter. "I thought you had a place in town."

"We weren't planning on staying long," Niall says, grabbing a wooden chair from the kitchen table. Placing it at the edge of the carpeted section of the room, he then sits down and proceeds to fidget with the zipper of his windbreaker.

I stare out the large, rectangular window to my left. The trees and dense forest surround us past the yard like a thick, evergreen cloak. It's strange how its tightness comforts me in a time like this.

Marcas clears his throat when he enters the room; Sam and Finn follow close behind. Sam leans against a doorframe behind Niall's chair while Finn sits on a pine-green couch against the far wall. Jamie gets up and moves to his side.

Marcas holds my gaze for a moment with his furrowed brow creased so deeply that I wonder if it will leave a permanent indentation. Then he turns and paces the length of the room.

"Marcas . . . please," I say, quivering slightly, clearing the worry from my throat.

"Seriously, who were those guys?" Jamie adds.

As if to torture us, Marcas takes long steps back and forth for a minute before he stops in front of me.

Not liking the conflict I see heavy in his eyes, I gulp down my anxiety.

"Dude, just tell them," Finn says, holding Jamie's hand tightly.

"Like a band-aid, man, rip it off. Shae can take it," Sam agrees.

Marcas kneels by my side, leaning in close. It causes me to instinctively do likewise. I hold my breath.

"Please!" I beg in a whisper. "Were they with Brad or not?"

"No." Marcas' eyes shadow over as if not being Brad is not as good news as one would hope.

I nod and hold back tears because I don't think I can handle another psycho guy out to get me.

Marcas cups my cheek in his hand and wipes a tear away with his thumb. "Please don't do that. I promise it will be ok."

"Tell me." I gulp down the fear lifting from the pit of my stomach. "What's going on?"

"Shae, I need you to know—my promise to you—I meant to keep it," he says as if he had already failed. "But I also gave my word not to speak of what I am about to, no matter the cost." His green eyes shimmer with concern as he searches mine for understanding, but I am so on edge that I can't even blink. "I promise, I'll tell you everything."

My heart suddenly sputters in my chest. Now. Now I get my answers.

"Those men are here because of me, not Brad," Marcas says quietly.

"You brought them here?" Jamie blurts out, spinning to look at Finn. "You knew who that jerk was and didn't say anything?"

"No! I didn't know they were the same guy!" Finn exclaims.

"Conall has come for the same reason we have, but we did not invite him—had no idea what he had planned to do." Then Marcas looks back at me, his eyes full of sorrow. "I didn't know he would try to hurt you."

"Why are you here, Marcas?" I say, looking into his eyes. "That guy, he said—"

Marcas takes a deep breath. "I knew I'd have to answer that someday." He smiles slightly, his eyebrows subtly raised, yet his voice remains semi-serious.

"Not home builders, I take it?" I smile awkwardly through my unease because, for just one meager second, I want to believe what he is about to tell me is as simple and unscary as a pile of bricks.

The pensive look he gives in return confirms I'm about to be disappointed.

My leg bounces wildly, my heel patting rapidly on the floor to the beat of my heart. I am afraid—afraid of everything changing and having no way of stopping it.

65

Marcas stands. "What I am about to say will sound absurd, made up even, and probably impossible to believe," then he starts pacing again. "But it is all true."

I hold my breath, unsure if I am really ready to hear what he's been wanting to tell me all along.

"No joke, you guys can't tell anyone," Niall chimes.

"Niall, seriously?" Jamie glares.

He snarls back at her, but she ignores him.

"Just say it, Marcas," I say.

Marcas comes to my side, and with the back of his fingers, he strokes my cheek lovingly. "It is hard to explain." His hand comes to rest on my shoulder. "But it has to do with your necklace."

As if signaling *I am here*, the pendant warms against my chest like it had done so many times before.

"My necklace?" I say, feeling it through my shirt, hesitant to reveal it. "What does it have to do with any of this?"

Marcas grins knowingly. "Everything, Shae—it's the very reason my brothers and I are here."

CHAPTER 4

No More Secrets

For a moment, I stare at Marcas in disbelief.

"You're here because of this?" I repeat as I pull the necklace out from under my collar.

Marcas smiles and says, "Yes," as he beckons me for it.

It feels abnormally warm in my hand as I unclasp the chain and slide it into his open hand. I feel naked—vulnerable without it.

"How do you know it?" I ask, swallowing hard, watching him flip the pendant over and caress the etchings on the back that only I knew were there.

"I would know this anywhere," he replies quietly. "It belonged to our mother."

A wave of shock hits me hard in the chest. I look at Finn, Niall, and Sam. They must secretly hate me for keeping it all this time.

"Wait a minute, that necklace? The one you helped fix? Marcas, why wouldn't you say something—tell her? You knew and—"

"It wasn't the time," Marcas says, looking at me.

Guilt almost drowns me. "I'm sorry, Marcas." My throat tightens. "I didn't know. I found it in the woods and—"

"Shhh, Shae, it's alright," he says as he reaches for my hand as though to give it back.

Pulling away, I cry, "Marcas, no, I couldn't possibly take—"

"Yes, you can!" Retaking my hand, he piles the chain in the center of my palm, the pendant resting on top. Then he gently closes my fingers around it, his hands wrapping around mine. "Trust me. It's meant for you."

Niall lets out a snorted laugh. "Sheesh, it wasn't easy to find, though."

"Yeah, hidden right under our noses." Sam winks.

How can they be all right with this?

Guilt weighs heavily as I watch Marcas closely. How can I keep something of their mother's that means so much to them that they would look for months to find? And yet, in my hands, I hold the necklace tightly, thankful to still call it my own.

Like a slow-moving picture, the vivid image of the woman from my dream drifts into my mind. It is as if I am back in the forest, her standing before me. She is holding the necklace—Marcas' mother's necklace. She looks at me with the same vibrant, golden-rimmed emerald eyes and warm smile that Marcas has. How could I not have noticed it before?

"I saw her," I say quietly, almost afraid to say it aloud. It is insane even to think it. How—how could I possibly dream about their mother?

"She was standing in a meadow—flowers all around us."

"Who was?" Jamie asks.

I look at Marcas instead. His knowing grin widens, making my heart leap in my chest. Through his eyes, I see his mother's bright, sweet smile staring back at me. For a moment, I hold on to the reality of the dream—a chance to meet Marcas' mother. Something I will never be able to do again. I don't know how it happened or why, but I can't fight the truthfulness I feel in it.

"She was so beautiful," I say breathlessly.

"Shae, who are—"

"Our mother," Marcas says to Jamie without taking his eyes off me.

"How did you—I thought she was—"

"In a dream, Jamie," I say. "She reached out to me, wanting me to follow her."

"And you did," Niall says eagerly. "didn't you?"

"Shhh!" Jamie, Finn, and Sam growl at once.

"Just let her tell it!" Jamie says heatedly, even though she was ready to play a round of twenty questions moments ago.

Niall scowls but stays silent.

"Not at first," I continue. "Another woman came and—"

"Another?" Marcas asks sharply, looking at Sam, who only shrugs back. Marcas' rigid brow deepens. "Did you know her?"

"No. But I think your mother did," I say, recalling the worry in her eyes and the panic in her voice; it sends chills down my arms, even now. "The woman was angry; she ran at us. Your mom insisted I take the necklace—she gave me no choice! She put it on me, and I ran—so fast. The other woman chased me. She was right behind me! I almost didn't get away."

I feel a gentle hand on my shoulder, and I look up.

Marcas gives me a slight grin, though his eyes are troubled. "We believe it was a vision, not a dream, that you experienced."

As soon as he says it, it all makes perfect sense. How real it felt; I knew it had to be more than a dream.

"But why show me a vision I don't understand?" I ask. "Why give me the necklace and not to the other woman who obviously wanted it?"

70

"Because our mother chose you," Marcas explains. "She must have seen something worthy in you enough to pass it on to you willingly."

"But how did she see it? When?" I exclaim. "Did you leave it up there for me to find?"

"No," Marcas says somberly. "All I know is I was sent here to find the necklace—to find you."

Heaviness builds in my stomach as a chill of unease shifts in the room.

"Who? Who sent you, Marcas?"

"My people," he replies. "There's so much more to this than the necklace; that's what I've been trying to tell you!"

"But you haven't told me anything! Who are they? How—how do they even know who I am?" The rapid intake of breath makes me light-headed.

"We are forest people," Marcas says, moving to the center of the room, his hands fidgeting with the cuff of his folded sleeve, his back to me. "Ireland is full of folklore, dating back centuries," he says quietly. "Some call it shape-shifting." Marcas turns around slowly. "We call it Fáelad." He looks to Jamie and me for proof of understanding, but we only stare back rigidly. Marcas clears his throat. "Meaning wolf-shape."

Silence fills the room.

Jamie suddenly laughs. "*Ahhh,* you guys." She points to them all and shakes her head. "Boy, you had

me good there for a second. Shape-shifting wolves."
She laughs again, but no one else joins in.

A large lump forms in my throat. The wolves—in the forest!

Marcas looks at me; his sad green eyes, thick with concern, connect with mine. A tingling feeling starts on my arms and travels down my spine like a slow-moving surge of energy. Deep down, I know Marcas enough to know he believes what he says to be true.

"Wait!" Jamie gasps, her smile fading. "You're serious? Please, Finn, tell me you're joking, right?"

"They're not," I whisper, keeping my eyes on Marcas. They are the only words I can muster, all the rest frozen in a storm of truth and fantasy, borders blurring by the second. But it is enough; Marcas smiles.

Like the mist from my dream, the others in the room dissolve away, leaving only Marcas and me behind. As though a single strand of light connects us, I concentrate on Marcas' features, imagining the creature residing inside him, the one who had saved me that day in the forest.

But how did I become part of this seemingly imaginary world without ever realizing it? How could they keep something this epic from us so easily?

"Werewolves?" Sam snorts. "Those things aren't even real."

"We're both human and wolf, not one controlled by the other," Finn says, caressing Jamie's hand.

"And that's different; how?" Jamie scoffs as she tries to tug her hand away, but Finn won't let go.

"That full moon garb is a load of crap." Sam chimes in again. "We choose when we change, not some lunar cycle."

Seeing Jamie ease up a little, Finn kisses her hand. "We don't hurt people. You don't have to be afraid." Then he smiles when she doesn't pull away again.

"We can't even turn people into what we are," Niall adds. "We're born this way."

Marcas' eyes, heavy with worry, beckon me to come to him. I want to—to show him I'm not scared. But I am terrified. Not of what he is, but of the world I have known my whole life, having lived in and trusted. How could it lie to me, trick me at a time like this?

Marcas' eyes slowly dim, and he turns away.

"Marcas," I say, rushing to him.

"I wanted to tell you," he whispers, "but didn't know how."

"Marcas, I'm here—see, right here!" He shakes his head, and my heart aches. "I don't care. You hear me? I don't care what you are!"

His sorrowful eyes pierce mine when he looks at me, and my breath catches.

"You're scared; I see you are!"

I kiss him hard, then again. Staring into his eyes, I

73

say, "Not one bit," followed by another kiss.

"You say that now, but when you know it all, you'll—"

"Run—I swear I won't."

"Damn it!" he growls. "This isn't how I wanted this to happen."

"Shhh, Marcas, I know. It's alright."

He just stands there when I wrap my arms around him; I try not to question why. Then, slowly, his arms find their way around me, hugging me so tight I think he'll crush my ribs. Then, with his kiss on my lips, I feel the electrifying passion in all of me.

"But what does this all have to do with that jerk in Anaconda?" Jamie asks.

When Marcas puts his forehead against mine, he breathes a weighted breath. "I think maybe that's enough for now."

"No!" Jamie and I blurt out.

Marcas presses his lips together. "Conall," he says quietly. "He wants the necklace."

"But he didn't know I had it until today. He came to the shop and harassed Jamie to find me. Why?"

Marcas' shoulders drop. "They were the wolves who attacked you."

I feel the color drain from my face; my legs wobble. They've been stalking me! All this time, I thought the worst of that day was behind me.

"Shae was attacked!" Jamie screeches, her eyes

74

wide.

"Jamie, I'm sorry. I didn't try to keep it from you; it's just—"

"No!" she says, leaning forward, pointing her finger at me. "You said it was nothing! You should have told me the truth!" she yells louder, bitterness sharp on her tongue. "You could have been killed!"

Tears well in my eyes, but she only glares hard at me and sits back with a huff.

With her arms folded across her chest, she looks away. "We always tell each other everything," she mutters to Finn, but I'm sure it is meant for me. "I am her best friend, for crap's sake."

Finn draws her close and whispers something in her ear, and she nods but remains troubled.

Marcas leans over to kiss my cheek. The pine and sandalwood scent clinging to his shirt soothes my frazzled nerves, but not enough to end the ache in my chest.

"Why—why would he—" I stammer.

"Convenience," Marcas replies plainly.

"Oh, that makes me feel loads better!" I scowl hard, my stomach twisting and turning into tight knots. "He tried to kill me, Marcas!"

"I would never imply his actions to be justified," Marcas retorts. "I only explain the reason for the attack."

"We tried to get there as fast as we could," Niall

75

chimes in. "Did what we could to protect you."

Yes! Yes, they did. And I know I owe them my life, even more so now that I know Conall has been stalking me like prey. But how Marcas said it made me feel like a literal piece of meat.

I take a peek at Jamie. Having been watching me, she quickly looks away, her eyes glaring coldly at the worn cupboards in the kitchen.

My anger dissolves away. Tears try to puddle in my eyes, but I repeatedly blink to hold them back.

Jamie means everything to me, and even though it hurts, I'm willing to give her all the time she needs if it means she will eventually forgive me.

"How did you know where to find me?" I finally ask, looking at Marcas.

"Yours and my connection through the necklace led us to you," Marcas says, "though I didn't realize it at the time."

"It told you where to find me?" I say, astounded.

"I sensed you were in danger; I felt your fear and your pain as if they were my own."

"It's how Marcas knew you needed him that night at Duke's, too," Niall adds.

Marcas squeezes my hand softly. "I'm sorry. We had no way of knowing Conall would react this way when we saved you."

"No, of course not. How could you?" I say, though, I am still not thrilled about it.

"Can you feel . . . other feelings?" I ask shyly, the skin in my cheeks heating up.

Marcas' lips form into a smirk. "I feel a pull toward you. Feelings I've never felt before. Strong. Powerful. Electrifying. I had to be near you."

My cheeks flush hotter as a smile breaks out for all to see.

Suddenly aware we're not alone, I drop my gaze and tuck a strand of hair behind my ear. "So, um, so why can't I feel your emotions?"

Marcas' cheeks grow a rosy shade of pink, too, something I have yet to see.

"Your pendant is an amulet—forged in magic," Marcas says, taking my hand and guiding me back to the loveseat. "A direct link to our family bloodline, passed down through generations, though much of its powers remain a mystery.

'Our parents weren't just any Fáelad; they were royalty," Marcas continues, returning to the center of the room. "Wolf rulers over every forest on this continent, keeping peace and harmony like the ones who came before them."

"Wow, princes? Seriously?" Jamie asks eagerly. "Not bad," she adds, grinning at Finn. He smiles and then kisses her.

"When a clan queen dies, her amulet, the source of all her strength and power, vanishes," Marcas continues, "only to reappear when the next rightful

77

heir is ready to claim it."

The words queen and amulet freeze in my mind. He couldn't possibly mean that—

"Shae's a queen?" Jamie gasps.

"Yes, finally!" Niall grins triumphantly. "Man, it feels so good to say that out loud."

"Will be," Sam corrects.

"But how?" I say, looking at Marcas. "I'm not like you!"

"Neither was our mother," Marcas says, smiling warmly. "It's how the magic works, linking the best of both species together."

Grabbing a folding chair, Marcas sets it up beside me, then reaches for my hand. Like delicate petals of a flower, he lifts each of my fingers slowly, revealing the amulet underneath. His touch sends fiery sparks through my body; it makes me want to feel more.

"These markings." He points to the etchings on the surface of one side of the amulet as he inches closer to me, "speak of a maiden on a journey following the growth of these four trees." He gently moves his pointer finger along them one at a time. "The Oak for strength and nobility, the Elder for transition and continuation, the Aspen for transformation." He stops on the last and looks at me. His eyes sparkle with excitement. "And Heather for romance and love."

My breath catches in my throat as I look into his

eyes.

"When you put the necklace on, you triggered the dormant power inside it. Our mother's wolf lineage then transferred to you through the shared vision."

"I'm a wolf?" I gasp.

"It's why your arm and other injuries healed so fast." Sam declares. "You're not one of us entirely, but I guess enough to reap some rewards."

They all look at me expecting a response, but my thoughts and emotions are fighting against each other so much that I can't think straight.

"Don't be too mad at him," Niall says. "He could only sense the amulet, not who had it. We didn't know it would be you we were looking for."

"Which is why it took so long to find," Finn says.

"Has to do with the future King proving he's worthy," Sam adds.

"King?" I whisper in surprise at Marcas.

Marcas watches me tensely. "I wanted to tell you, but it was forbidden," he says softly, holding my hand tighter. "I couldn't stand the idea of my destiny existing without you. It haunted my every thought: to never see you again, to never be close to you—never touch you. It was maddening."

"Maddening." I chuckle a little. "I'm beginning to see the connection."

"I tried to stay away, but fighting your hold on me was too hard; the pull to be with you was too strong. I knew how much I would end up hurting you if we got too close. I didn't want to be near you if I couldn't be with you. It hurt too much."

I nod and breathe out a breath I feel like I have been holding in for weeks. Jamie was right; Marcas cared too much for me and freaked out.

I smile at him, hoping he sees how much his words have meant to me. Not to mention feeling the thrill of such a confession.

"Here," he says, taking the necklace from my hand and attaching it around my neck, then smiles. "Back where it belongs."

I touch it; its smooth surface feels like home.

"When I saw you had the necklace." He touches the amulet softly. "I stayed away, worried you'd reject me after how I treated you."

"You should have told me." I frown, "the second you knew."

"I know." He lifts my hand and kisses it, a slight droop at the corner of his lips. "But I'm afraid that's not all."

I swallow hard, not liking the tepid look in his eyes.

"My duty as the future king was to not only find the amulet and find you but also to maintain the balance and peace between the forest and the human world; to do that, a marriage must occur by the next full moon."

80

"Marry?" The word catches in my throat like a wad of stale bread.

"I know it's sudden."

"Sudden?" I breathe hard, unable to get enough air into my lungs. "We haven't even been together a day, Marcas!"

"You think I want to do it like this? To not date you as you deserve? No! Not at all how I wanted it. But I can't change what's happened."

"I don't see why we have to rush into this!"

"Because of Conall," Sam says heatedly. "He's hell-bent on ruining everything."

After seeing Marcas give Sam a stern stare, my stomach flips. "What? What aren't you telling me?"

"Nothing you need to worry about. We can handle it," Marcas says.

"No, Marcas, I want to know! He's not here just for a necklace, is he?" The knots in my stomach twist tighter.

"No." Marcas finally says, his thick tone unnerving me.

"Tell me." I breathe. "All of it."

"Tomorrow, please, you've been through enough."

I stare hard at him, unwavering in my demand. I will not back down. I want to know everything, regardless of how bad it is. And by the look of angst Marcas is giving me, it will be.

Finally, Marcas nods his head. "You are the key to

81

everything," he says, caressing my hand. "You hold the possibility of peace for our kind or our destruction."

I suddenly feel ill and have to close my eyes, the room spinning.

"We are not without enemies." Marcas rises from his seat again and paces the room. The action sends warning chills up my spine. "And some would like nothing more than to destroy what we've built, Conall being one of them."

"Why would he want that?" Jamie asks, shifting her eyes on me for a brief moment.

Marcas sighs heavily. "Conall's father, Daragh, and our father, Riordan, used to be best friends; they did everything together. He even went with our father to search for the amulet when it was his time to find it. But unfortunately, they ended up falling for the same woman."

"Our mother, Roisin." Niall says.

"Daragh grew jealous, wanting our father to find the amulet and the heir and leave Roisin to him."

"A lot like you two; they didn't even know she'd already found it." Niall snickers.

"When Daragh learned of this, he was outraged," Marcas continues, "and soon devised a plan to steal Roisin away from my father and take her for his own."

"Like father, like son," Sam spits out under his breath.

"One of our father's most loyal servants overheard

82

talk of Daragh's plans, leaving our father with no choice but to banish his best friend forever.

'Daragh later drilled his hatred into the hearts of his sons, the eldest being Conall. Even after his father had died, Conall refused to let it go, secretly plotting his revenge. However, in the end, he was unsuccessful," Marcas says, a hint of a tear glistening in his eye, "for our father died of natural causes."

Jamie huffs. "Makes sense why he hates you so much."

"Makes even more sense why he's so desperate to attack even with Marcas around," Sam clarifies further as he moves to the kitchen table and sits down.

"Conall said *other* wolves can sense the amulet. Is that true?" I ask.

The boys nod.

"Well, that stinks." Jamie snarls. "But if you're supposed to find it, then why does anyone else have to know about it?"

"Equal rights to the crown," Marcas says firmly. "If I am to be a king, I must fight for it or lose it to one more worthy. There is no privilege of birthright with the Fáelad. It is implied, but not guaranteed. Should another wed Shae, they would lead in my stead, her by their side until death."

"Being a hybrid, it would take a *very* long time," Finn says sadly.

83

Shudders of fear lodge in my chest as I clear the lump of dread from my throat. "Is that all of it?"

Marcas frowns, "Sorry, love."

My body tenses. "How much more?" I ask.

"Enough to complicate things," he says, coming over to me.

"More than making Shae marry some loser?" Jamie asks. I look at her timidly as she looks at me, a weary smile across her face.

"There are rebels out there willing to end noble rule altogether," Marcas relays. "To do this, they must kill the future queen before the marriage ceremony is performed, thus throwing our world into unimaginable anarchy."

"Geeze." Jamie snarls. "Don't tell her that!"

I gasp, and his hand grips mine tightly as he crouches down. "I will not let that happen," he says hurriedly. "You have my word."

"He's blunt for a reason," Sam says sharply, his eyes dark with trepidation, a look I'm not used to seeing on him. "Trust me; you don't want to see these guys like that. It would be hell on earth."

"Sam's right," Niall adds, "Without our restrictions, it would be a carnal-instinct overload; every human an easy target. We can't let that happen at any cost!"

"I thought you said you don't hurt people!" Jamie retorts.

84

"It's rare," Marcas counters, "but if one does not honor me as their king, our laws are seen as breakable."

"Conall?" I say as I fight back the tears.

"The very threat we face," Marcas says, stroking my face. "But I will not let him come near you!"

Conall's words of warning flash in my head, and my chest tightens, making it difficult to breathe. Bending over, I rest my face in my hands.

"Please, Mo Chroi." Marcas puts his hand on my shoulder and pulls me in, wrapping his arms around me. "Tell me—what can I do?"

I shake my head slowly, not knowing how to answer such a loaded question. There are so many factors involved; so many things to go wrong.

I clench my eyes and bury my face in Marcas' warm body.

Why me? Why now? Destiny? By chance? How could all this be happening when only a few short weeks ago, my only concern was a broken heart?

All I know is that, dead or alive, my fate rests in the protective hands of Marcas and his brothers. And once again, my future is chosen for me.

CHAPTER 5

Trials And Error

A red-breasted robin perched on the wooden railing out the living room window pecks at a juicy worm clutched in its talons while rain drizzles down on it. For some reason, I find it fascinating to watch.

During the night, a storm had come, bringing with it low temperatures and dark, gloomy clouds. Outside, the steady rain pings off the metal roof in a methodical rhythm while the house inside remains still.

The clock on the wall clicks loudly when the gears shift to 6:30 a.m.

As I sit on the couch with my legs stretched out to the other end, cold air seeps through the systematic holes in the rough, techno-colored afghan wrapped around me from my chin to my freezing toes.

The unfamiliarity of the house makes me long for the comfort of my own home, Tax by my side. I worry about him there all alone for too long. But Marcas and the others had insisted I stay the night, believing it unsafe for me out there anymore. How can one sleep knowing that?

I squeeze my dry, bloodshot eyes shut tight and try to blink the sting away to focus through my fatigue on the bird again.

Even with Marcas' warm arms of security wrapped around me, I could not drown out the endless drums of thoughts, worries, and fears that echoed in my mind. When 2 a.m. had approached, Marcas went out to stand watch in the forest, skirting the house while images of Conall's face continued to haunt my dreams, his words repeating in my mind.

Eventually, I gave up and came out to the couch; sleep did not join me.

"Can't sleep?" A voice comes from the kitchen, startling me. Sam removes the lid of a metal thermos and fills it with steaming coffee.

I breathe out and pull my knees to my chest. "Nope. You?"

"A few hours. But Marcas wanted me to relieve him before you got up. Guess that didn't work out, did it? You want some?" He nods to the thermos as he

87

screws the lid back on.

I shake my head.

"You okay? You went through a lot yesterday," he continues as he grabs snacks from the cupboard over the sink.

I shrug and try to smile, but to be convincing would take more energy than I have to give.

"It's a lot to take in, I know. Marcas worried telling you all at once might be too much to handle."

"Maybe just a little," I say with a slight smirk. "But I guess he didn't have much choice, did he?"

"You're not thinking about leaving, are you?" Sam asks, watching me more intently. I find his concern unexpected. "I know, *forever* with the big stud sounds overwhelming—high-strung, hard to handle—you know what I mean." He winks. "But he's a good guy. And besides, we like having you around."

"Hard to handle, huh?" Marcas says quietly from the hall as he steps into the room, wiping water from his hair with a towel. As he pats down his disheveled hair, he tries to shove Sam playfully, but Sam darts to the side and swirls around the corner before going out of the room, thermos in hand.

Marcas lays the towel on the back of the kitchen chair and smiles at me. "Mo Chroi, you're not supposed to be up yet."

I smile back, unable to hide my excitement at hearing him call me by his pet name again.

"You know, it's hard to shut your brain off when your boyfriend tells you he's a wolf, among other crazy things."

He sits beside me and rests his chiseled chin on my bent knees.

"Sorry about the timing," he says thoughtfully, then grins, his adorable dimples popping into play. "But I tried to warn you."

My smirk falters. "I know."

"How are you holding up? Did you get some sleep?"

I shrug.

I don't want to tell him how freaked out I am, but I'm afraid I can't hide anything from him now, even if I want to. He can feel how I feel without me saying a word.

He gently tucks a loose strand of hair behind my ear. "You mad at me? I won't blame you if you are." With his eyes bright and smile wide, he leans over and kisses me before I can reply.

I have never been more thankful for Niall having found me an extra toothbrush before bed.

Marcas leans back and stares knowingly at me.

I breathe out forcefully. "I thought we'd have more time. I don't want to rush into anything or be forced to do something I'm not comfortable with or ready for."

"You never answered Sam's question." Marcas'

eyes dance with trepidation even though his smile tries to hide it. "Have you decided, then?"

A prick of unease shifts inside me as I look down at my lap; so many thoughts run through my head, overwhelming me with uncertainty.

Marcas slowly sits back. "I see." His smile fades as a look of forlornity replaces it.

"Marcas, wait, I—"

"No, it makes sense," he says softly yet weighted with defeat. "I knew it would be too much. You said it wouldn't . . . but I knew."

"No, that's not it."

"Shae, I get it," he says forcefully, though his eyes are sad. "You don't need to say it." He then gets up from the couch, using my knee to steady himself. "I should get some rest. You should too."

"Wait—Marcas." I grab his arm and try to pull him back down. "Let's talk about this!" but his legs lock where he stands, facing away from me. I can feel his body pulling against me, withdrawing from me physically and emotionally.

"Please!" I beg.

He just stands there, thinking, who knows what, and it hurts my heart. But no matter what he thinks, I will not let go; I won't let him walk out on me, on us, again.

"Please, Marcas, sit down."

Reluctantly, he finally does but faces away, resting

his elbow on the arm of the couch. I shift closer to him and sit cross-legged, facing the side of his body, my lower half still under the blanket.

"Marcas, don't be like this. Give me a chance to explain myself. You owe me at least that much."

He looks at me from the corner of his eye, his face unreadable, then looks away again.

"I didn't mean to—you just caught me off guard, is all." I lean toward him, placing my hand on his thigh. "And I don't think it's fair that you're mad at me right now with all that's happened."

"No, you're right," he says firmly. "I don't have the right to get angry." His foot starts tapping rapidly on the ground. "But when the woman I love decides I'm not enough—that this is too much—I think I have a right to be upset about it."

The word love does not escape my notice, but now is not the time to address it.

"That's not what I was—" Frustrated, I take a second to clarify my thoughts. "Look, things for us haven't gone very well, right? Stuff neither one of us wanted to have happen, happened. You have to agree; that's a lot to handle all at once."

Marcas nods his head, but his body remains stiff.

"And not to bring it up again, but your erratic behavior was confusing and sometimes downright mean. So, you can't blame me for being a little cautious."

He squirms slightly, and I know he wants to retort but refrains. His willingness to handle this with restraint makes my heart burn with optimism. It means he feels sure enough about us to not let his emotions get the best of him.

He looks away, shaking his head. "I know I was awful—hurtful. I made your life miserable, but I said I was sorry." His voice is stern when he adds, "You can't still hold that against me."

I watch him, seeing the pain I am causing him, and it kills me.

"Marcas, I don't. I understand how hard it must have been for you and can only imagine the stress you've been under. The unrelenting responsibility of it all—knowing that the fate of your people is so exposed like that." I pause, knowing my following words will sting. "But I never asked to be in the middle of it."

He shakes his head and mumbles, "It's too much to ask of you, I know."

His statement breaks my heart and makes me want to forget my bewildered mind and let my love take over, but I can't. I have to make him see that no matter what, if I stay, it will be my choice to do so, not because of a threat to my life, not because of some mystical relic I found in the forest. Not his mother's choice; mine.

"I don't want you to misunderstand me; I care

92

about you so much. I just need you to—"

"Shae, I get it—this is way more than you ever asked for, and it's selfish of me to even have you consider it. Even when you said you wouldn't run, I knew—"

"That's not fair. I feel like I don't have a choice about this, and that scares me. I've had my future planned for me once before, and I don't like the feeling."

He looks at me, his sorrowful eyes on the verge of tears. He exhales and nods. "And I get that too."

"If I stay, I want it to be because I want to, not because I'm *destined* to."

"I know," he says, looking away once more. I can feel him slipping away again.

"I heard everything you said last night. Every scary detail. But I'm still here—right now, with you! But you can't expect me to act like everything is okay because it's not. Not by a long shot."

He nods again.

"But I also saw *you* last night—the real you," I say softly. "Caring, compassionate, loyal—loving. And then everything changed for me—my future, how I feel about you—about us." Leaning closer to him, I touch his arm. "I care deeply for you, Marcas. Amulet or not, I feel things for you I never thought I could for anyone, especially after—"

He looks at me sharply as if I said something

93

wrong, but I understand when I see his eyes shimmer with wetness.

"I—"

"Don't! "I quickly shake my head. "I know, Marcas, you didn't mean to."

"But now you question me, question all this. I never wanted it to be like this." He puts his hand on mine on his arm and squeezes as he gives me a sorrowful smile, a tear streaming down his cheek. "I will spend the rest of my life making it up to you if you'll let me."

I reach over and wipe his cheek, and he grabs my hand and holds it there as he looks deep into my eyes.

His touch and gorgeous green, emotion-filled eyes make me love him even more.

"All I ask is you give me time to process everything," I say quietly.

He nods and sniffs as he looks down at our hands. He sighs again as if extinguishing his heartache. "You take all the time you need. I'm not going anywhere."

"Good." I smile so full of love that there is no way he will ever question again how much I care for him.

But then I can't help but circle back around. "So, you love me?" I say with a smirk; my head caulked to the side.

His cheeks turn bright red, the edges of his lips slowly turning up. "I thought that part was obvious. Shae, I—"

94

Grabbing his face, I draw his lips to mine. His kisses are soft and affectionate; with them, I desperately want our problems to melt away and let our relationship bloom. But I know it is not possible.

He pulls back and smiles, his green eyes sparkling as he takes my hand and interlocks our fingers before resting his head on my shoulder. "Don't scare me like that again," he says, exhaling slowly.

"I'll try not to," I reply softly.

We sit for a while, my fingers combing through his silky, black locks while his arms hug me; we let the moment carry us away.

*　　*　　*

Marcas and I wake to the sounds of pots and pans being banged together repeatedly. The cupboard doors in the kitchen are open, their contents scattered across the countertops.

"Sorry for the noise," Finn huffs. "I can't find—did you use my skillet?"

"Sam," Marcas groans, stretching, "burned his dinner on it two nights ago, I think."

"I'm gonna kill him," Finn growls through gritted teeth as he marches from the room. Loud shouting floats down the hall, followed by the pounding of feet as Finn chases Sam through the house, down the stairs, and into the yard. I can still hear them yelling

95

even outside.

"Look who's awake," Jamie says, entering the living room from one of the side rooms. "About time you sleepyheads woke up."

The coo-coo clock on the wall crows once.

"Give them a break." Niall smirks as he comes out of his bedroom across the hall from the kitchen. "They've been busy getting to know each other better."

Marcas and I share a subtle look of knowing.

Sitting on the chair across from us, Jamie begins picking at her hair, plucking split ends like petals on a daisy, while Niall pulls a loaf of bread from a breadbox on the counter.

"What happened here?" he asks, looking for a place to make lunch. I smile and point down the hall.

"Serves you right," Finn bickers as he enters the room. "You owe me a new pan!"

"Don't hold your breath," Sam mumbles, dabbing the trickle of crimson blood from his swollen lip with the back of his hand as he slumps sulkily down on the green couch.

Finn smiles at Marcas and me, then exchanges cute glances with Jamie before going into the kitchen and putting things back together.

Other than the quick smile at Finn, Jamie continues to weave her fingers through her hair.

"So, what's the deal? We stickin' around here or

96

what?" Niall asks while using a huge butterknife to slather crunchy peanut butter on one piece of bread before drizzling honey on another. He smashes the two together and takes a large bite as he sits on a chair at the table.

"Shae and I agree she should stay here until we figure things out." Marcas quickly peeks at me for confirmation, and I smile back. And then he looks at Jamie. "It might be best for you to stay too. If you want."

"I'm cool with it! I don't work until Monday." Jamie says, giving a coy smile at Finn, who gives her one back as he flips a grilled cheese sandwich on the griddle.

"Sam, you and Finn can take her into town to get a few things. Then swing by Shae's."

"Bring Tax back, too," I say hurriedly, glancing at Marcas. He smiles, then looks at Sam.

"Yeah, sure, whatever," Sam says, yawning widely.

"Don't forget his leash," I add to Jamie, who nods.

From the end-table drawer, Jamie grabs a pen. "Hey, grab her something to write on, would ya?" she says, snapping her fingers at Niall.

Niall mumbles with a mouth full of sandwich, something about being a servant, as he stomps over and hands me a piece of paper. It has a greasy smear of peanut butter on the corner from his messy fingers.

The playful banter and typical family interactions

97

make things almost seem normal, as if last night never happened. But I know everything is far from it. Marcas wasn't letting on last night at how dangerous Conall and the others are, but I know what I saw in Conall's eyes and his evil grin.

He'll stop at nothing to get me, including hurting everyone I care about if they get in the way.

Putting those thoughts out of my mind, I make my list of clothes, toiletries, and dog food as I nibble anxiously at my thumbnail.

Marcas comes over and puts his hand on my shoulder. "You still doing okay?" he says with a look of concern.

Shrugging, I give a delicate smirk, "But I'll figure it out."

"You're doing it again." He smiles. Leaning over, he kisses me. As he rises up, a soft yet troubled look remains in his eyes, then he walks into the kitchen, snatches the hot sandwich off Finn's plate when his back is turned, and quickly darts out of the room.

"Hey, who took my sandwich?" Finn exclaims, having turned around to find the plate empty. He picks it up as if it could be hidden underneath. Jamie and I giggle as he scours the rest of the kitchen like a madman.

"Are you really okay?" Jamie asks me.

I give her a pointed eyebrow and motion toward the hall with my head. We get up and move in that

98

direction.

"I mean it; who took it?"

Jamie and I both shrug, showing our empty hands as we pass.

"Sam!"

"Yeah, sure," Sam says flatly. "I stole your cheesy sandwich with my super go-go gadget arms and scarfed the hot mess in two seconds flat."

I laugh, believing he would have if he'd had the chance first.

Finn eyes Niall, who pipes up quickly, "Don't look at me."

We leave the bickering boys and go down the hall past the bathroom, where the shower is running and the Foo Fighters' 'The Pretender' is playing.

Once inside Marcas' unoccupied room, I close the door. The sparsely furnished room holds only a queen-sized bed and a nightstand with a four-inch wolf figurine sitting on top of it, which I hadn't seen in the dark of night. A keepsake or ironic gag gift from his brother, perhaps?

"Finally!" Jamie says, plopping on the unmade bed. "I've been waiting all morning!"

"So, you're not still mad?"

She looks at me, sadness in her eyes. "Of course not. I knew I should have asked more about your arm, but I was too busy being selfish. I'm *such* a jerk."

"Jamie, no, I should have just told you."

"Yeah, well anyway, I'm sorry for how I acted last night. I was just mad at myself for not seeing something wrong—again."

I sit beside her on the bed and wrap my arms around her. She squeezes me tight before letting go and shaking her head. "That must have been so scary for you."

I give a slight nod.

"And how are you feeling about all the rest of it?"

"Numb mostly."

"Yeah, I guess that makes sense." She pauses. "Hey, just curious, you think if Finn and I were to get married, I'd be a wolf princess?"

I can't help but chuckle at her thought process, but at the same time, I wonder, "Is that even what you want?"

"I don't know," she says, trailing off. "How do you feel about becoming their queen?"

"Like I want to run from the house screaming and never looking back," I say sarcastically. "I knew they were keeping secrets, but I never imagined—"

"Wolves? Yeah, me neither." She sighs and watches me for a moment.

"You don't want any of it? Not even Marcas?"

I don't answer; still so overwhelmed I don't know where to begin.

"You're saying *no* to him?"

"Jamie." I point my brow at her. "It's more

complicated than that."

"It doesn't have to be if you don't want it to."

She's right. If I strip it down to whether I care about Marcas, the answer is definitely yes. Do I see a future with him? Also, yes.

"I'm mostly upset about the scary stalker guy after me."

"Aside from that, do you care about Marcas?"

"Of course I do." I smile. But then it turns into a grimace. "I'm just not happy about everything else."

Jamie lies back on the bed and rests her arms behind her head. "You're so lucky."

"Is that what you call it?" I scoff back, joining her, our heads side by side.

"I mean it. You get the guy, you'll be royalty, and hey, maybe you'll even get to wear an extravagantly jewel-encrusted crown! Wouldn't that be something?"

"You forget the part about me not even being *me* anymore!"

"Wolf or not, you're still you. That won't change, no matter what your DNA's made of."

"What about Conall? What if he gets to me? I'd be either his stupid wife, tortured by the fact I will never see Marcas again, or he'll just kill me and end my misery quickly. That's not even considering any other deranged wolf plotting against us."

"Marcas would never let Conall or anyone else put their grubby hands on you."

101

"I know, but what if—"

"Shae, stop!" she says, propping up on her bent elbow facing me. "Don't ask for trouble where there isn't any. Trust that hunk of a man of yours, who would do just about anything for you, and everything will work out. Even a blind person can see that—the way he stares at you with his big puppy-dog eyes." She sits up further and bats her eyelashes as she puts her hands up, mimicking swooning gestures.

"He doesn't do that!" I grab the nearest pillow and smack her across the face with it.

With her mouth open in playful shock, she grabs the closest pillow and repeatedly bashes me with it.

With fits of laughter and girlish screaming bouncing off the walls, we tumble off the bed, our pillows flying as we land on the floor with a thud, staticky hair clinging to our faces.

I don't care if it's juvenile; it's just the right amount of innocent fun I need to relieve my stress, if only for the moment.

"Do you think everything will be ok?" I ask as our laughter subsides.

Winded, Jamie collapsed on her back next to me in the middle of the floor. "With four incredible guys protecting you? Chances look pretty good."

"I mean it; don't you worry Finn might get hurt?"

"Yes, but he can handle himself." She smiles, but it doesn't reach her eyes. "And if not, he'll have three

102

brothers to back him up. That, I'm sure of."

"Jamie, stop trying to be tough and be honest with me. It scares you to death, right? Because it does me! I'm the reason this is all happening. And if something were to happen to any of them—"

"It won't!" She rests her head on my shoulder. "We're all in this together, remember?"

I lock my arm with hers, and we stare at the textured ceiling like a starry night sky. "You'd make a gorgeous princess, by the way."

"You bet I would!" she says triumphantly.

We are still laughing when the bedroom door opens. In nothing but a skimpy, white towel wrapped around his waist, Marcas stops in the doorway, his eyes wide with surprise, to find us lying on the floor.

"Ladies?"

Tiny droplets of water glisten on his muscular shoulders and travel down his chiseled chest, then come to rest in the creases of his abs before trickling further to the towel below.

"Hellooooo, dolly!" Jamie ogles him as she covers my eyes with her hands. "Too steamy, sweets. You're not supposed to see that." She laughs as I try to push her hands away.

"Very funny," Marcas says, drying his hair with another small towel. He tosses it on the bed and moves to the dresser, not caring if he is mostly naked in a room with two women.

"Finn, come get your woman; she's gawking at my man," I yell, laughing.

"Jamie, get your butt out of there," Finn calls from the kitchen.

With a large grin, she slaps my arm, jumps to her feet, and whizzes past Marcas into the hall.

I get up and head for the door myself but am blocked by Marcas.

"Where do you think you're going?" he asks, his voice deep and seductive with playful undertones.

I put my hand on his wet chest, his body still hot from the shower. "I'm not staying while you get dressed." I smile wide.

"What kind of man do you take me for?" His eyes beam mischievously. "I only wanted one of these." He touches my chin and slowly draws my face to his. I savor his woodsy, earthy scent as his lips touch mine. His gentle kisses turn hungry; I respond as if I'm starving, too, my arms wrapping around his neck. His arms encircle me, pulling me tightly against him. Water seeps from the towel through my clothes as desire seeps into every fiber of my body.

Finally, I pull away before our appetite for more moves us toward the bed. But my arms remain around his neck.

"Has anyone ever told you what an incredible kisser you are?" he whispers, his breath tickling my neck.

"Hey, love birds, we're leaving," Sam hollers from the front door, saving me from having to answer Marcas' humiliating rhetorical question.

I leave the room and join the others so Marcas can dress. He comes out a minute later wearing dark jeans and pulling a red shirt over his head.

While Jamie shoves her smiling face in mine, I playfully push her back as I retrieve the folded list from my back pocket, then slap it into her open hand.

"Don't forget to check in, especially if you see anything suspicious," Marcas advises with a stern look at Finn first, then lingers longer on Sam. "Be careful, and get back as soon as you can."

"We need to stop for food, so we might be longer," Finn says before following Jamie out the door.

"Don't worry, bro," Sam says, slapping Marcas on the shoulder as he walks by. "We'll keep our wolf senses on high alert." He winks at me before going out and down the stairs.

"I'm serious, Sam; no messing around!" Marcas hollers down at him.

Sam gives a thumbs up over his shoulder.

While Jamie waves from the back seat as they drive away, Marcas puts his arm around my shoulders at the top of the stairs and, in a quiet, happy voice, says, "I like that you call me your man."

My cheeks burn red, and when I look up at him, he kisses my lips gently, seductively making my body flush with excitement.

CHAPTER 6

Too Much Time

Finn, Sam, and Jamie had only been gone for half an hour before boredom set in.

I tried to distract myself with reading, but the only books in the cabin were a handful of encyclopedias, books on auto mechanics, and an old bible. None of which presented optimal distracting capabilities.

Marcas was no good to me either, preoccupied with making phone calls on the balcony outside. And Niall, let's just say he takes longer to get ready than Jamie.

Eventually, Niall found his way into the light of day.

Niall shuffles the cards; they glide in synchronization from an arch formation back into a stack.

After winning the first two rounds of Rummy—I argue by cheating, though he denies it—I make him shuffle the deck twice as many times, then cut it in half again for good measure.

While he puts the deck in the center of the table and flips the first card over to start the discard pile, I align all suits in my hand and plan my strategy.

The two of hearts is there for the taking.

A sinister grin of utter domination shrouds Niall's face. His eyes narrow in on me as he anxiously taps his fingers on the table.

"You can go now—any time." He grins.

"I'll go when I'm good and ready!" I tease, flashing him a snarly glare.

I look at my hand again as if, by some miracle, the cards have changed; nope, they still stink, so I swipe a card from the top of the deck, add it to my hand, and then discard the four of clubs.

Faster than I can blink, Niall snatches it up and puts it with his cards. When he discards the queen of hearts, the corners of his lips curl up slyly.

Grumbling under my breath, I slowly reach for the queen.

"You sure you want to do that?" Niall smirks as though he knows something I don't. It sends me into a spiral, second-guessing every ounce of strategy I think I have.

"Hey, Niall, do you have any more siblings back home?" I ask, stalling.

Munching on a pretzel, he stops mid-bite and chews a little slower. "Umm," he mumbles. "We had a sister once. Vevina." He shifts the cards in his hand several times. "She'd be eighteen now." Though his tone is upbeat, sadness hides in his eye.

"The other woman from my vision—could she be your sister?"

He looks over his cards at me with eyes deep in thought and then shakes his head. "Not possible."

The question of 'why not' lingers in my mind. The women resemble each other too much to not be related. But I don't dare dig any further and risk upsetting Niall.

"Sorry," I say, watching him pick at his cards.

He puts them face down on the table, then groans as he stretches his hands high over his head. "For what?" he grunts.

"Bringing her up."

"Eh, in the past," he says, picking up his cards again. "Besides, we have you now, right?"

I agree with a smile, though I know better than to believe the loss of his sister means so little to him.

"Tell me about your dad; what was he like?" I ask, discarding the four of diamonds.

"Oh, he was the best! Tall, strong, loyal—just an awesome leader, you know? Everyone loved him. Marcas reminds me of him sometimes, especially in the last few weeks." He glances over my shoulder at Marcas, sprawled on the loveseat by the window, reading a book he must have found elsewhere. Niall then adds a little quieter, "Not as serious, though. But I don't blame him; the last seventy-five years have been significantly more challenging for him than for our father when he was Marcas' age.

I swallow hard, forcing unchewed pretzels to scrape as they go down. "I'm sorry—did you just say seventy-five *yearz*?"

"Oops." Niall grimaces, "Probably shouldn't have said that." He then laughs.

"Seriously? You can't just say something like that and not explain! How old are you guys really?"

"Hmm, well, I know I'm sixteen, and Marcas—twenty-four." His smile widens as he chews.

"Niall!"

He gloats while looking at his cards as if the conversation isn't happening.

"Marcas?" I raise my voice over my shoulder, a large, saccharine smile forming on my face. I make sure Niall sees it.

Reaching over the table, Niall grabs my hand, the cards in it bending. *"No!"* he mouths, shaking his head vigorously as he smirks. *"Don't you even dare!"*

110

"Yes, Mo Chroi," Marcas asks after a moment.

"Tell me," I mouth, a lingering sinister smile remaining on my face as my left eyebrow lifts to a point.

Niall squeezes my hand tighter.

"Are you getting hungry? We have some pretzels here." I smile smugly.

"Oh uh, no, you go ahead," Marcas says lazily.

"Ok, they're here if you want some."

He doesn't respond.

"That's cheating," Niall grumbles, pelting me with several pretzels.

"Ooh, you better watch it," I warn, counter-firing with a few of my own. One strikes Niall in the forehead and ricochets off, hitting the wall. We have to muffle our laughter so we don't disturb Marcas.

"I tried to warn you. Don't start what you can't win," I taunt as I pick pretzels off the table and viciously bite them in half. "Go on; it's your turn."

While taking a drink, Niall flings the ten of spades onto the discard pile, but it flies beyond it, drifting to the floor.

I pick it up and add it to my hand rather than on its intended mark.

"So?"

"Marcas' right; you don't let up, do you?" Niall laughs.

Eyeing him, I threaten to chuck another pretzel at

111

him.

"Ok, fine," he whispers, "but you better act dumb if he brings it up later!"

I nod and discard another card.

"So, Marcas isn't technically twenty-four—he's ninety-eight."

"*Wha?*" I gasp loudly, then slap my hand over my mouth.

"Yeah, crazy, right? Basically, one year for us is four years for you." He then picks up my discard and takes a drink of his soda.

"Yikes! That makes you, what, like, sixty-four? Talk about being a senior!"

Soda sprays from Niall's mouth as he tries to keep from laughing. I muffle my own hard laugh into a napkin. Our shoulders bob as we fight back the urge to laugh out loud.

I glance back at Marcas. His book rests on his chest, eyes peacefully closed.

Niall mops up the sticky mess with a towel, puts it by the sink, and sits back down. Then, with a slight flick of the wrist, he fans out all his cards save one, face-up on the table, and discards the last before folding his arms triumphantly.

"Ah, crap. Niall, you suck," I say, throwing my cards on the table.

"Again?"

"Sure, why not. It can't get any worse than losing

for a fourth time."

He shrugs his shoulders while stacking the cards, then hands them to me.

"Okay, wait—if you're that old, why do you look so young?" I ask as I begin shuffling.

"Aging kind of comes in spurts, each time making us look more grown up than before. The last one happens at around 17 or 18 human years. It's like you're a teenager one minute, then transformed into a twenty-year-old practically overnight. It's kind of cool, actually. It hurts like a mother, but at this point, I'm so sick of this." He points to his scrawny adolescent body and rolls his eyes. "I'd go through it tonight if I could. But I can't, so I wait."

"What triggers it?"

"Don't know. It just happens when it wants to."

"And so, you go through high school over and over for what, like twelve years?" I ask, trying to shuffle the stiff, slippery new cards that keep flicking out of line. I have to repeatedly tap them back into alignment.

"Pretty much—acting like an immature doofus while I wait."

I laugh, not for a second believing his awkwardness is an act.

"Ugh, I think I'd stick to the forest."

"Ok, so it's not so bad. Sometimes I get lucky and meet a few people who make it worthwhile.

113

Sometimes I even meet someone," he says with blushing cheeks.

"Oh really?" I grin. "Is that what everyone else does?"

"Are you asking me if Marcas has had girlfriends besides you and Maggie? He smirks. "He's almost a hundred; what do you think?"

Sneering at the mention of her name, I huff, "Well, yeah, I figured as much, but what about the whole destiny thing? If he's supposed to take his father's place from birth, why even date? What would be the point?"

Realizing what I've just asked, my heart sinks. I've never once thought about how Marcas must be feeling about all of this. Has his heart been broken by a love he can't have, ripped from each other's arms because of a destiny he never had a say in?

Niall says something to me, but his words jumble together—noise my sidetracked brain can't decipher.

I've been naïve to assume I would be Marcas's first choice. Did he think of another when close to me?

"Shae, are you ok?" Niall asks when the cards in my hand scatter across the table. "Dang it, I upset you again, didn't I? I knew I shouldn't have said anything."

"It's all right," I say slowly, picking up the mess. "Just thought of something I hadn't before."

"Yeah, because of something I said. Marcas is

going to kill me."

"Stop; it's not your fault."

A loud buzz sounds from the living room. Marcas struggles on the couch, trying to reach the phone in his back pocket.

"Sam? Sam, are you there?" He looks over at us, breathing rapidly. "It just cut out." The phone rings again. "Sam? Are you guys okay?"

Loud talking comes back, but I can't make anything out.

"Dang it, slow down. I can't understand you." Marcas touches a button on the screen and places the phone on the table in front of Niall and me. "You're on speaker."

"Can you hear me?" Sam yells as if he's an old, deaf man.

"Yes," Niall and I say together. Marcas puts his hands on my shoulders just as Niall gives me a weary look.

"K, good, because I don't want to repeat myself a bunch of times. Shae's cabin's been—" A loud shuffling sound comes through, like someone is wiping something over the mic.

"Sam?" Marcas huffs. "Sam?"

"Sorry, dropped the phone," Sam yells. "We got to Shae's place; the front door's been bashed in."

"Tax?" I gasp.

"He's not inside. Jamie found a broken collar and

115

some blood spots on the porch. It's not much, probably just a scratch. We'll keep looking for him, though."

My body stiffens, the chill of dread blanketing me.

"Marcas, the place is trashed. Whoever did it isn't messing around. They even cut up the mattress in the bedroom."

"It's Tavis, Conall's go-to guy!" Niall whispers with contempt. "He loves to mutilate whatever he can get his hands on."

Kneeling beside me, Marcas puts his hand over mine, holding it tightly. "Please, don't worry, they'll find him." Then he shoots Niall a disappointed look I don't think I'm supposed to see.

"Sam, that's enough. Grab what you can and get out of there. I don't want to risk them staking the place out. And make sure you get the front door back on so no one asks questions."

I rest my head against Marcas' chest as he continues to talk with Sam. His muffled voice vibrates my face. Finally, he hangs up and converses further with Niall; all the while, I silently pray for Tax.

"Out-outside, please," I sputter.

Lifting me up, Marcas leads me outside, down the stairs to the plastic lounge chair under the deck, and then goes back inside, returning a minute later with a blanket, bottled water, and a handful of oblong candies. He puts them in my hand, and I pop one in my mouth without thinking. Then I smile as the buttered popcorn flavor devours my tastebuds. So, Marcas did leave them on my car after all.

Even without a breeze blowing, it is still cool in the shade. As Marcas covers my legs with the blanket and hands me another handful of jelly beans, I watch a squirrel run around the base of a large tree across the yard, scurrying in and out of hiding places, searching for food. I find myself wishing I could be a squirrel; my biggest worry—whether I'd have enough food for the winter. But then I recoil, remembering how often I'd seen them mushed on the side of the road.

Marcas pulls the blanket further up on my chest and stands there, watching me. "I'm losing you again, aren't I?"

I look up at him and smile warmly, "Never."

"Sam volunteered to stay behind while the others head to the store. Sam will find Tax, and he will be ok. I'm sure of it."

"When do you think they broke in?" I can't help but imagine Tax wandering around hurt all night in the cold.

"Most likely just before dawn," he says, looking out into the yard. "Conall is sending us a message. He's too smart to think we'd let you go home alone."

"What kind of message? Ps: you're next!"

"Shae, please don't worry about this. We won't let

117

anything happen to you; I promise."

I nod but don't believe in such a promise, not when so many factors are at play.

My mind shifts to what Niall had said just before the phone call, and my body instinctively trembles.

"Shae, you're cold. Let's go back inside where it's warm."

I shake my head. "I want to stay. I like it out here.

"Mind if I join you?"

I move my legs to the side, allowing him to sit.

"Marcas, can I ask you something?"

"Anything, Mo Chroi,"

"It's kind of personal," I warn.

Marcas' eyes dance with concern as a weary smile crosses his lips.

"And I'm not sure how to ask, so I'm going to just come out with it." I take a deep breath. "Is there . . . someone else?"

"Besides Conall? At this point, there's no real way of knowing who—"

"Not him." I raise an eyebrow. "I mean, like Maggie."

He blinks several times, his confounded brow deepening.

I sigh, unsure how to word it without sounding like a ridiculous, jealous girlfriend.

"You know." I shift in my seat, looking down. "Some lost love, back home, pining over you."

Suddenly, he flings his head back and laughs robustly.

"Stop laughing! It's not funny, Marcas. I'm serious!"

"I'm sorry, Mo Chroi, but you are absolutely adorable when you're jealous." He smiles as his laughter fades, his eyes gleaming with tears.

"I'm *not* jealous!" I huff, slapping his hand. He quickly grabs it in midair and brings it to his chest, where his heart resides.

"I think it's sweet—you being worried about another woman," he says more seriously, a smile lingering on his lips. "But don't be. There has never been anyone else, not seriously, anyway."

"Since we're on the topic—why Maggie?"

His smile disappears. "Shae, you don't want to hear about that."

"Yes, actually I do!"

"Right, and the second I say something you don't like, you'll get mad at me."

"No, I won't, I swear."

He gives me a *'we'll see about that'* sort of look as he shifts his leg on the lounge chair so he can look at me head-on. "You have to understand; I wasn't in a good place when I met her. We'd recently moved to town, and my future was imminent. And hiding from it seemed to be a good option at the time. It sounds cold, but she kept me distracted; for a short while

119

anyway." He lifts my hand and kisses it, then smiles sincerely. "I assure you; she meant nothing."

Now I don't know whether to be elated or upset that he so easily dismissed Maggie and what they had. I mean, I am happy to hear she was just a distraction, but at the same time, could I be too?

I force a smile, but I can't keep it in place.

Seeing it, he frowns. "Don't you even—you promised!"

"No, I know," I say quietly, trying to give another smile. "Honestly, I'm not mad."

"But you are upset," he replies, with a look of genuine concern. "And I don't want you to be."

"Not about Maggie, per se, just—are you sure I am who you want?"

Marcas' eyes narrow, his brow creased deep. "I know I haven't made it easy for you to trust me, but I would never lie to you or deceive you with how I feel about you. You have to know that!"

"But you kind of did," I say, realizing it sounds harsher than it did in my head.

Marcas sighs long and hard, making my stomach tighten.

Dang it, Shae, keep those stupid comments to yourself!

"Not because I wanted to trick you into being with me. I would never do that!" Marcas finally says, his voice constricted. "I was only trying to spare us the heartache of falling for each other when being together wasn't possible."

"I'm not naïve, Marcas. I know you've had two lifetimes' worth of experiences with women."

"Who told you that?" Marcas bocks.

I snarl. "Niall. But don't blame him. I made him tell me."

"I will not apologize for having a life before we met, Shae, however long that may have been, but I—"

"That's not what—I just want to know if there's someone you loved but were forbidden to be with." I sigh, looking away as I bite my nail. "Because of the amulet thing?"

"Never. Not one." He strokes my cheek with the back of his fingers and pulls my hand away from my mouth. "My destiny—cliché as that sounds—gave me the very person I've wanted from the moment I met her. Not Maggie, not someone back home, no one but you. And if I had known you were waiting for me, I would have never wasted a moment fighting against what was meant to be."

I squeeze his hand in mine. He smiles at me, and my heart skips.

"I will never stop trying to show you that I am yours, always and forever."

"I felt it too." I breathe out as a surge of electricity pulsates from the roots of my hair to the tips of my toes. "When we met—it was more intense, more potent than anything I've ever felt before. It scared me

121

at first. I don't even think I knew what real love was like until I felt it for you."

Reaching over, Marcas draws me into a kiss. They are gentle yet compelling, as if to thank me for loving him.

My lips tingle when he stops.

"Now that's what a guy likes to hear." He grins coyly, resting his forehead against mine while gazing into my eyes. He kisses me again, then rotates us on the lounger so we snuggle together in each other's arms.

We live in our little moment for a while, feeling the raw, real, honest emotions that have come of it. That is until the return of the reality of our annoying predicament sends a suffocating wave of angst washing over me.

"I hate that jerk, Conall. He needs to just give up," I say grudgingly. "I don't want to die just because he fights for revenge, or power, or whatever."

"Don't talk like that. There will be no dying!"

Marcas speaks with such conviction I almost believe him. He squeezes me for added assurance.

"My father was the greatest warrior I have ever known. He taught me everything—how to fight and provide for my people. How to find you, keep you safe, and rule by your side when the time comes. But as my loving father, he taught me that the most important thing would be our bond—strengthened by the

122

amulet, not be there because of it. That alone convinces me we have a fighting chance. I know what we have is unbreakable. Not by Conall. Not anyone."

"You truly believe that?"

"With every ounce of me," he says with a cocky grin. "As far back as I can remember, there has always been a struggle with those insisting on destroying the peace our ancestors created. And like those before us, we will prevail in stopping them."

"But at what cost? The life of one of your brothers? Of yours? I can't let that happen. I just found you. No way am I letting you go!"

"Shhh, Mo Chroi." He draws me close and kisses my forehead softly. "I am quite capable of protecting everyone, as well as myself." I feel the smile on his lips against my skin.

Shifting, I rest my head against his chest and watch the setting sun darken the yard. His heart beats steadily, comforting me against the unknown.

"So, what do we do now?" I ask, with an exhale that holds its weight in uncertainty.

"I kind of like what we're doing." He gently rubs his hand down the length of my arm.

I chuckle. "I meant about Conall."

"All we can do is wait. I left messages for the other clans and await their reply. Some I doubt will."

"How many others?"

"Five kings in all."

"That many!"

He nods. "It used to feel excessive, all crammed together in one place, but once Ireland cultivated the lands, we were forced to find homes elsewhere."

"Where did everyone go?"

"South America. Africa. All over the European and Asian countries, as far south as Indonesia. My family came here."

"Every part of the world," I say, astounded.

"Some argue there's not enough of us now to maintain the peace and order necessary for us to stay hidden from the human world. Even going so far as to request official voting on the matter."

'Who decides that? Is there a leader of the kings?"

"Aye, a woman." Marcas smiles. "But not just any woman." He winks. "The queen of the fairies."

"Now you're just making things up."

His grin broadens, neither confirming nor denying it.

"Collectively, we counsel together for the best interest of our kind." He speaks reverently, delicately stroking my arms as though he is just like me, but his words say otherwise. "In times like these, it is best to notify all of them regardless of the outcome."

"If it's in everyone's best interest to handle a rough traitor like Conall, why wouldn't they respond?"

Marcas laughs lightheartedly but confidently.

124

"Conall is trouble, but nothing we can't handle. Contacting others is more of a precaution and a willingness to keep everyone aware of the situation rather than a necessity. If they choose to assist, I welcome their wisdom, insight, and, if freely given, a few men. Otherwise, we're on our own."

His explanation doesn't sit well with me one bit. What good are allies if they do nothing to aid in times like these?

"Why not send for your own men, then? There has to be more than just your brothers, right?" I say, looking up at him.

"Many more, but us being here as long as we have, our defenses have already been divided enough. And I need as many loyal warriors as possible defending our land." He shifts his body again, his tone more serious. "There are other threats out there besides Conall. My appointed regent, the one who also served my father, keeps order in my absence, though I don't know for how much longer."

"The same guy who told your father about Conall's dad?"

"One in the same."

What a heartbreaking story. To lose your best friend in such a way? I don't know how I would survive if Jamie was no longer in my life. I cringe to think of such a fate.

"So, tell me about this whole changing thing?" I

125

ask, needing to change the subject to keep the depressing idea from burrowing into my mood.

His hand stops stroking my arm momentarily. Hesitation about the topic or being uncomfortable because of it—I don't know which.

"Sorry, should I not have asked that? I don't know the rules or—"

"No, you should know." His hand starts moving again and then rests on mine, squeezing it gently. "I just sometimes forget you're actually mine."

His words, his tone, and the love I feel electrifying through his hand on mine make my heart patter rapidly in my chest. I wonder if he can feel it.

"I've kept these secrets for so long; it's hard to remember that I can tell you about them now."

"It's okay if you're not ready."

With an upbeat, happier tone, he says, "Nope, ask away."

"Ok, well, how does it all work? You change forms in the forests, right? Never in towns? What if a town's in the forest?"

"Instinct tells us where we can and can't change; similar to how the amulet's powers bind to you, it binds us to the forests. When we're in wolf form, anyway."

"It's magic?"

Marcas nods. "It protects humans from some of our kind who don't live by the rules and keeps us safe from humans willing to destroy what we've created."

"So, why hide us here? We're smack dab in the middle of a forest."

"The house is magically protected by a big half-acre bubble. The Fáelad can't take true form within its walls. See that log there? Just before the yard's border, it becomes a gray area."

I let out a long sigh, the questions in my head dissipating for the moment.

"It sure is pretty out here."

He smiles and squeezes me close. "I know what you mean."

My thoughts drift away with the evening breeze as I enjoy watching the setting sun's rays streak through the clouds, turning the sky into a masterpiece of light oranges, dark blues, and grays.

"What's it like being a wolf?" I ask without considering how personal the question might be.

"Perfect." Marcas pauses, his hands holding mine again. "Nothing in the human world can even remotely compare. I feel empowered by the forest, free to do as I please. Sleeping under the stars every night, feeling the wind in my fur, and sensing the trees swish by when I run. It's so unbelievably exhilarating."

"Sounds incredible. You ever think about staying a wolf and never changing back?"

"Sometimes, I guess. But I like living in both

worlds. The human touch is well worth the return." He looks down at me with a smug smile.

He is so sexy I can't resist the pull to kiss him, and so I do, adding "smoothtalker" afterward with a smile.

"Years and years of practice," he says with a knowing grin.

"Very funny," I jeer playfully, shoving him away.

"What?" He laughs harder. "You don't like that I bring experience to the table?" He pulls me close again as if to show me how much he knows with a kiss.

"Don't even!" I use my arm to block him, like a shield. "You keep those manly ways away from me!" I laugh, trying to playfully glare at him.

"You afraid you can't resist it?"

I know I can't, but he doesn't need to know that. "You're wasting your time. It won't work on me!"

"We'll see about that." He moves in closer, and just as his seductive lips reach mine, a car's bright lights blast through the trees, flooding our faces with light.

Niall comes thumping down the steps and stops next to us. "Cut that out or get a room." He smirks and hands Marcas his phone, then quickly clears his throat when Marcas scowls at him. "They, um, called and said they were on their way. You left your phone upstairs."

I slap Niall on the leg, sending a loud smack into

the night. He winces and grabs his leg in mock pain.

When Jamie and Finn get out of the car, Marcas goes to greet them.

"Sorry we didn't get to finish the game." I look at Niall as the others start to unload groceries.

"That's ok. You get things figured out with Marcas; maybe talk about what was bothering you before? You know you can always tell me; I'm a great listener, and I mean about *anything*!" He raises and lowers his eyebrows rapidly.

"What? No!" I gasp. "Don't make me smack you again," I warn, swatting the area near his leg.

"Ewe, I'm kidding," he says, dodging my swings. "That's what your girlfriends are for."

While Jamie opens the front seat and grabs her purse, she calls for Niall to help with the groceries. He eyes her passively in return.

"What?" She glares, "I do the shopping, not the unloading."

"Fine," he huffs and goes to help.

"Everything ok?" I ask her as she stops next to me.

She flashes me a troubled look, forcing a sinking sensation to shift in the pit of my stomach.

"I have to tell you something; you're not gonna like it." She folds her arms tightly to her chest. Because of the chill in the air or her news, I can't tell.

"Is it Tax?" I gulp, panic fluttering to life in my

129

chest.

She shakes her head slowly while looking down. "You forgot to take out the garbage, and now your house smells like a rotting pile of dung." She then lets a coy smile surface as she plops onto the lounge chair beside me, biting into a red licorice rope triumphantly.

"You brat, I thought it was something horrible."

"It is! I'd seriously send a hazmat team in to take care of it before moving back in."

Walking past with both arms full of white grocery bags, Marcas smiles at us as Finn and Niall get more from the trunk.

"Hey, where's Sam?" I ask Jamie.

"Niall didn't tell you? Sam found Tax under a porch down the street after we left. They should be back any time. The poor thing has a cut on his leg, but he'll be fine."

"But how are they—"

"Your car. You don't mind, do you? We needed another ride."

"I guess wolves don't usually need a car, do they?" Despite all my conversations about it, it still slips my mind.

She shrugs and stands. "You coming?" She jerks her head toward the stairs. "Finn's making lasagna casserole with big chunks of sausage and stewed tomatoes. I told him we'd help with the garlic bread."

130

"I'll be there in a sec. I want to wait for Sam and Tax."

She places her hand on my shoulder. "Don't be too long. It's getting dark, and it's not safe."

"I won't," I say quietly, laying my head against the lounge chair, watching the forest road leading away from the yard and out of sight.

CHAPTER 7

Company

Standing in the center of the moonlight in the living room with the afghan from the couch draped around my shoulders, I look out the window, the unknown keeping me awake.

Finn is presently keeping watch outside somewhere. There has been no sign of Conall or his friends since the cabin incident, but Niall says their silence only means they are planning something.

Everyone else is fast asleep; the only sounds are the tree branches scraping against the house as the wind wildly blows and the clock tick, tick, ticking on the wall.

Tax walks up to me and rubs his cold, damp nose

against my dangling hand, then sniffs and nuzzles it until I scratch his ears. Jamie had been right about his cut being shallow. Though it is already on the mend, I can't shake the worry. And Sam saying Tax wouldn't have gotten away if Conall's men had been in true form hadn't helped my nerves, either.

Outside, the full moon illuminates everything, causing dark shadows to dance back and forth along the thick tree line bordering the yard.

Uneasiness stirs.

As my eyes scan along the grounds, movement at a break in the trees sends my heart into a palpitating frenzy. Three wolves step onto the grass, stopping at the log Marcas said the gray area began.

Marcas is at my side in seconds. "Shae, what is it?" he asks, pulling me against his warm body. I raise my shaking hand and point to the window. He steps forward and looks out.

When he turns back around, he kisses the top of my head. "Stay inside," he says assuredly, then goes down the hall and yells for Sam and Niall while pounding on their doors on the way outside.

"What's going on?" Jamie asks sleepily as she wraps a silky bathrobe over her skimpy shorts and tank top, her hair as picture-perfect as the rest of her.

"Wolves," I finally manage to whisper. "In the yard."

She gasps, her hand shaking as she covers her

mouth.

Niall comes in between us, putting his arms around our shoulders. "Wha'd I miss?" he yawns.

I nudge my head toward the window.

He leans forward slightly. "Ah, it's fine; they won't hurt us."

"You can't know that!" Jamie clutches my arm. "Finn's out there somewhere."

Sam joins us at the window and looks out, a smirk on his face. "Course we can," he says in a deeper than-usual lack-of-sleep voice, "We read minds," and taps his temple, eyeing me creepily, then winks.

Feeling a different kind of worry, I gulp down hard.

"I can't believe you're older than me!" Niall snorts. "Don't listen to him; it doesn't work like that."

Sam shrugs as Niall glares at him.

"We hear what's directed at us and nothing more," Niall says, squeezing Jamie and me closer to him. I know she is freaked when she doesn't shove him away.

"Think mind reader, but with bad reception, at least when we're human." Niall smirks. "Like a radio station out of range, but most of the time, it's enough to get the point across."

Jamie clutches my wrist tighter. I can feel my hands swelling from loss of circulation. I know what she's thinking—will their wild world of wolves and magic ever get easier to fathom?

134

"Who are they?" Jamie asks quietly.

"King Tynan's sons. Their father must have sent them," Sam says thoughtfully as he waves into the night. "Look! See, Finn's right there!" He points to the edge of the forest. "He's just fine."

Releasing her grip on me, Jamie runs to the window, cupping her hands on the glass to see through the glare of the hall light behind us.

"Stay with the girls. I'm going down," Sam orders Niall before leaving the room.

I move closer to Jamie by the window and look out. Silhouettes of people stand where I had once seen the beasts.

"You okay, Shae?" Niall asks as he comes closer, leaning on the window's edge. I give a distorted smile, and he frowns. "I promise they won't hurt you."

"They're not enough."

"Trust me, these guys can take care of themselves."

"They're coming inside," Jamie squeals as she ties the silky robe belt and scurries over to the kitchen table, trying to act casual by leaning against it.

Talking and laughter grow louder as the voices move up the porch steps and into the house.

"This place is a dump, Marcas!" a tall, attractive man with dark hair says sarcastically as he comes down the hall. "Couldn't you find a more suitable place to dwell?" Then, seeing Niall, he grins. "Niall,

135

my boy, how are you?"

"All right, Korin, and you?"

"Can't complain." The stranger's well-defined cheekbones and jawline harden like chiseled rock when his smile broadens. And although his eyes are dark and mysterious, they are full of warmth, making him appear as kind and friendly as his tone of voice implies.

Distant laughter moves in from outside. A moment later, Marcas enters the hall.

"It's not like we're trying to impress anyone." Finding me by the window, Marcas smiles, a look of curiosity shifting in his eyes.

A shorter, meatier-looking guy soon joins the room. With the help of his dark, spiky hair and the dim light, he appears menacing, his brown eyes darting around the room. They pause on me for a fraction of a second, then resume looking around.

The third companion is tall and slender, with large, muscular shoulders and forearms. He stares at me with gentle eyes the color of rich, creamy caramel and hair as light as the sand of the most beautiful beaches.

While they all congregate in the center of the room, Sam switches on the lamp in the far corner and the lights in the kitchen.

"This must be the beautiful creature you were telling me about," the tallest one says, spotting me by the window. He moves to take my hand. "The name is Korin." He bows and kisses the back of my hand. I look to Marcas, who suppresses a smirk when he sees me standing rigid.

"And these are my brothers." The man points with an open hand at the light-haired and dark-spikey-haired men, respectively.

"Hello, milady, Ardan, at your service." He places his hand over his heart, his light hair dangling freely in his face as he bows.

"Tate, ma'am," the last one says tight-lipped as he, too, bows before me.

"Hello," I reply, giving them a friendly smile even though I feel ridiculous as if I have walked into their cosplay without knowing how to act.

"Things are a bit cramped around here," Marcas says, moving to my side, "but the couches are comfy. There or anywhere else you can find a place. Foods in the fridge, bathroom down the hall on the left, and if we don't have what you need, there's a store in town. Other than that, make yourself at home."

"As you wish, milord." Korin smiles wide.

"Don't you even start." Marcas glares, giving Korin a friendly shove. "No formalities, I mean it."

Korin flashes me a genuine smile while trying to catch his balance. "Yeah, but what kind of friend would I be if I didn't give you crap for becoming king before me?"

Marcas seems more relaxed and carefree than I have ever seen him; I wonder why he keeps so much of himself hidden away.

When Finn finally comes in from outside, he makes a beeline for Jamie and the others at the table. She wraps her arms around his shoulders and hangs off him, smiling big. Adran then chuckles lightly as something Niall said. Tate remains quiet, sitting beside him, glaring.

Ardan appears friendly enough. But it is Tate's dark, on-edge sketchy demeanor that unsettles me, making the hairs on my arms tingle.

Sitting on the couch, I direct my thoughts to the window and the darkness beyond it, though with the lights on, I see only the reflected room more than anything else.

"How are you adjusting to everything?" Korin asks when he sits in the armchair beside me while Marcas joins the others by the table.

"I'm hangin' in there," I say with a half-smile.

"That bad, huh?"

Giving a shrug, I glance across the room at Marcas talking with Sam, Finn, and Ardan. "It's all happening so fast." I look back at Korin. "I'm sure Marcas told you about Conall."

Korin's pensive stare deepens. "Aye, troubling times indeed. It upsets Marcas greatly that he can't keep the danger from you." Then he smiles warmly.

138

"That's a good man you got there. A changed man; I saw it the moment I laid eyes on him." His grin widens, a sparkle in his eyes. "You've been good for him."

My cheeks burn from smiling as I blush even more. "So, um—are you to be a king too?" I ask, even though I already know the answer, but I dread further compliments.

"I am, but thankfully my parents are alive and well. Though the day will come soon enough. The way Marcas tells it, with the two of you, makes it sound very enticing."

A sputter of excitement rushes me. Marcas spoke of me to Korin; on more than one occasion?

"What kind of craziness is he filling your head with?" Marcas says as he walks up.

"That you dance like a one-legged pirate," Korin taunts back.

We all laugh.

Marcas pulls me to a stand and brings me in close. I can't help but smile at his laughing eyes.

Korin, having been watching us, is beaming.

"Come, my love, it's been another long day." Marcas wraps his arms around me gently. "We should let Korin and his brothers rest."

I nod

"Night, Korin." I smile. "Nice meeting you."

Korin bows his head again. "The pleasure's all

mine."

"Finn," Marcas calls over to the table. "Sam's finishing your watch, so get some rest. You too, Niall. There's plenty of time to catch up later."

Sam, Finn, and Niall nod and leave the room, with Jamie following them.

Holding my hand, Marcas guides me to his room and closes the door behind us. He removes his shirt, climbs under the covers, and pats the bed beside him. I look at him coyly, then eventually climb in. He wraps his arms around me as we lay facing each other, his arms holding me close.

For a moment, all is silent. But when Marcas' brow wrinkles and eyebrows pull together, it sends a feeling of concern into the pit of my stomach.

"Marcas, what's wrong?"

"What makes you think something is wrong?" he says quietly as he adjusts to get more comfortable. Or else he's squirming.

"Call it a hunch."

He takes a deep breath through his nose and lets it out slowly through his mouth, his breath smelling of mint. "It's Korin's father. He wants to discuss options."

"That's great!" I say excitedly.

Marcas breathes deep again, but this time he doesn't exhale.

"Right?"

"I suppose," he finally sighs. "But not here. Not anywhere Conall's prying eyes may see. Korin and I should only be a day or so." A strand of my hair moves back and forth, tickling my forehead with every puff of air from his words.

"Korin's the friend you told me about, isn't he?"

He nods.

"I can tell he cares about you a lot."

"You get that impression, do you?" He smiles again. "We've been through so much together—too much—He's practically family."

"I know the feelings," I say, thinking of Jamie.

"Even now, he struggles but still comes when I need him."

"With what?"

"Rebellion within his ranks."

"Like with Conall?"

"Worse. Family. Korin and Ardan are the oldest of five brothers, and Tate, the youngest. For whatever reason, Tate has never gotten along with his brothers, especially Ardan. He doesn't even try anymore to hide his dislike for the restrictions on our kind. Because of it, he and his father continue to bicker. I'm actually surprised to see him here."

"Why would he come then?" As unease creeps back into my mind, I use my nails to lightly scratch Marcas' back, weaving designs up and down and around his muscular shoulder blades.

141

"Whatever Tynan says, goes," Marcas says, winded as if my touch leaves him breathless. "If he told Tate to come, he'd have no choice but to obey." Marcas rests his chin against my forehead, his body relaxing further with every pass of my hand on his skin.

We grow silent.

As I continue running my fingers across his smooth back, I think about family betrayal. To loathe them enough to throw it all away; it's tragic.

Marcas' breathing slows, steady, and smooth.

"You'll be okay while I'm gone?" he asks as he plays with a lock of my hair, twirling it through his fingers. "I'd take you if I could, but—"

"Marcas, it's all right. If Tynan could help us, then do whatever he wants. I'll be fine."

"Where we're going, there's no reception," he says with a hint of aggravation. "You wouldn't be able to reach me even if you wanted to."

With his naked chest against my skin, feeling warm and inviting, I squeeze him closer, hoping the closeness will ease his discontent. Then I draw his face to mine, kissing him softly. Yet, as I pull back to look at him, his eyes still hold so much melancholy that it pains me.

"I'll miss you," I whisper and sigh, enjoying his tender touch as his fingers move through my hair. "Now, if you said you were going to some wolf party without me, I'd have to wring your neck."

He smiles. "What do you think you'll do while we're gone?"

"I don't know. But I know what I won't be doing, and that's playing cards with Niall—the big cheater!"

Marcas laughs, hugs me tight, then breathes close to my head as if smelling my hair.

"I don't know. . . ." I yawn. "Maybe I'll redecorate in here," I say, glancing at the empty walls. "Or better yet, if I get super bored, pick up some guys at Duke's. Seemed to work out for me the last time."

Slowly, Marcas shifts his head, staring up at the ceiling.

"Marcas, I'm kidding." A twinge of regret burrows into my chest. "Marcas?"

He eventually clears his throat. "I need you to be safe." His soft voice tightens as he speaks. "I can't have—"

"Marcas, I'll be fine like you said. And I promise I won't do anything stupid. So, please don't worry."

"But I will; every second I'm gone."

"I know." I breathe out, moving my face against his warm chest. His heart beats steadily in my ear.

As silence drifts in between us again, I wonder what will happen now that Marcas has found me. Will we get married soon? Not too soon, I hope. And how does one change into a full-fledged wolf? When will I? Will it hurt?

I sigh. "This secret stuff sounds like something

out of a movie."

His chest shakes as he laughs. "I suppose it does."

"And just a heads up, we need to talk when you get back."

"Well, that sounds ominous," he says, hugging me tight. "Am I in trouble or something?"

I laugh. "Just have about a hundred questions to ask you."

"In that case," he says, pretending to remove the covers and get out of bed.

I laugh and pull him back in, then kiss him passionately. "You're not going anywhere," I say, smiling, and then we fall back into place under the covers.

He pulls my face to his, "How about we discuss something else?" Then he smiles and presses his lips against mine. Each kiss feels soft, tender, and incredibly seductive.

When he finally releases me, I smirk at him, "You know you're pretty good at that."

"Really?" He leers mischievously, "You sure? I feel a little off my game. Here, let me try again." He chuckles as he reaches for me again.

Teasing, I pull away, but when I see the full-fledged desire in his eyes, I move in quickly, kissing him fervently. He inhales in surprise, then, without hesitation, joins in.

CHAPTER 8

Boys Will Be Boys

I awaken with a jolt to an empty bed, Marcas' side cold to the touch.

Robust noises come from the hall as I get up and open the door. Sam and Ardan are at the kitchen table arm wrestling while Finn leans over their hands, judging. Tate is on the couch in the corner, looking out the window, glaring as usual.

"Ardan, man, you got this," Niall yells as I walk over to the cupboard in the kitchen and grab a glass bowl out of it.

"Knock it off, Niall; I can't concentrate," Sam

hollers, then winces as the veins in his forearm bulge. Glancing over at me, he winks. Two seconds later, there's a loud thud as a hand slams down on the solid, wooden table.

"Yeah, man! In your face," Sam berates, pointing his finger at Ardan, then at Finn before torquing his body vigorously in a victory dance.

"Wait! *Wait* a sec! Sam," Finn calls over the noise. "Your elbow wasn't on the table!"

"What? Yes, it was!"

"Afraid not, dude."

"Take it back!"

"Fat chance, cheater!"

Sam grabs Finn in a headlock and wrestles him to the ground. "Take it back!" he grunts.

Arms and legs flop animatedly around as deep grunts and muffled curse words are tossed about.

"Never," Finn growls back.

Sam almost pinned Finn flat on the rug, his body sprawled over him, but with a quick leg jerk and a twist of his body, somehow Finn got away.

Niall and Ardan laugh hysterically while Finn sits on Sam's midsection, pinning his brother's arms to his sides with his knees, then proceeds to poke his collarbone at the base of his neck until he screams out his relent.

Niall, laughing, notices me and waves, then gets up and walks into the kitchen. "Hey, did you see that?"

"Mmm, hard to miss," I reply, suppressing the need to roll my eyes.

"How'd you sleep?"

"Better. You?"

"Like a baby. Well, except for when Sam and Ardan snuck in and taped me to the bed. I couldn't get out to go to the bathroom."

"Please don't tell me you peed yourself," I add, grabbing the cereal box beside me.

"I may be an animal, but I'm *not* wild!"

"Could have fooled me." I eye the commotion in the living room. "I'd hate to see what you guys were like when you were younger."

"We've always goofed around. Feels like old times."

I go about pouring milk into my bowl. "Where's Jamie?" Then I grab a spoon from the drawer.

"Outside with Marcas and Korin. She didn't like all the noise."

147

"Can't say that I blame her."

He smiles widely, "Hey, it's a house full of manly men; what do you expect?" and raises his arms, flexing his muscles to show off his nonexistent biceps.

"I have *no* idea," I add sarcastically as I take my bowl down the hall and out the front door.

A circular metal table and chairs sit on the deck overlooking the yard below. Marcas, Korin, and Jamie are standing in a semicircle, talking on the lawn. When I pull the heavy, metal chair from the table, it scrapes the wood, grinding loudly. All three of them look up at me. I awkwardly wave as I sit down. Jamie skips up the stairs to join me.

"What are you doing eating out here?" she asks, leaning on the back of an empty chair at the table. "It's cold out."

"Have you been in the house lately? Do you know what your boyfriend and the others are doing?"

"Enough said." She grimaces.

"What were you guys doing down there?" I ask with a mouth full of oat cereal.

"Korin's telling us about where he lives. Did you know he's from South America? So cool!"

"Marcas told me," I mumble, still chewing.

148

"His stories are amazing! Like a whole different world."

A smidge of jealousy pricks at me. I want to hear what it's like too.

"Korin said he and Marcas are leaving later," she says, sounding more like a question than a statement.

"I know," I say, chasing my cereal around in the bowl with my spoon, suddenly losing my appetite.

"Hey, come on, we'll find something to do. And before you know it, he'll be back in your cute, wittle, scrawny arms," she says, pinching my forearm.

I smile, though her humor does little to make me feel better.

She frowns, then looks at her watch. "Look, I'm here for you, really, but you think we can talk about this later? I need to jump in the shower before someone else does."

With a solid nod of affirmation from me, she smiles, pushes off the chair, and rushes inside.

Out of the corner of my eye, I spot Tate through the window sitting on the couch in the living room. At first, I don't see it, but as the clouds shift overhead, it exposes his scowl; lips pressed in a straight line, the muscles in his jaw clenched tightly, and his hard, beady eyes glaring at me as though the effort could burn a hole right through the glass.

Seeing me watching, he gives a grimacing smile before turning away.

The hairs on my arms and neck stand on end.

The more I think about Tate and his creepy ways, staying while Korin and Marcas go, the more my nerves prickle under my skin.

Marcas trusts him, but I'm not sure I can after what I just witnessed.

* * *

It is early afternoon when Marcas and Korin are ready to leave.

Marcas kisses me sweetly on the lips as everyone gathers around us outside. Jamie and Finn hold hands by my side. Niall and Arden are on the stairs, Tate on a chair under the porch, while Sam joins Korin, waiting to depart.

"I'll return as soon as possible," Marcas whispers to me.

The wind suddenly picks up, rustling the branches of the trees, the loud sound filling the silence with a hint of dread.

Drawing me close, Marcas wraps his arms around me. His smell I savor for as long as possible, wanting it to linger long after he's gone. It always comforts me, and I could use all I can get today.

"Sam, you're in charge," Marcas says over my head. "Whatever it takes, keep them safe."

Sam nods lazily. "No worries, bro," he adds as he smiles at me.

"Sam, no funny stuff, I mean it. Have Ardan and Tate rotate out, too." Marcas glances over at Korin, who nods once in agreement.

Ardan replies with a respectful nod, while Tate hardly even moves, which sends my insides turning with a feeling of foreboding. I hope Marcas is right about trusting Tate. If he's wrong—I don't want to think of the consequences such a mistake could bring.

"Marcas, you ready?" Korin beckons as he steps toward the edge of the property.

Keeping his eyes on me, Marcas says softly, "I am," and kisses my cheek tenderly. "I love you," he whispers before slowly moving away. A gust of bitter air rushes in, chilling me.

Every ounce of strength I have in me goes to

refraining from grabbing him and never letting go as he turns and follows Korin out of the yard.

Jamie interlocks arms with me. "He'll be fine," she says assuredly, though it doesn't make me feel that way. "Come on, let's go inside."

"So, what's the plan?" I ask, hesitant to take my eyes off the trees where the guys had disappeared through. She tugs my arm toward the stairs, and I follow.

"We could always lock the boys out of the house and have some peace and quiet for a change," she whispers with a smirk.

"I heard that," Finn yells from the top step, playing into our suspicions of superhuman canine hearing. We turn our heads together and giggle as we keep walking.

"You know your whispering is more like a dull roar, right?" he teases as he glances back at us. Just before we reach the top step, Finn grabs Jamie and whirls her into his arms as she screeches with glee.

Once again, I feel the prick of jealousy for what they have between them. They will never know the heartache of separation that a crown will cause, as is evident with Marcas' absence. But at the same time, for the first time today, I actually feel like smiling. If we are to get out of this whole Conall mess intact, I will have something I've never had before: brothers. And having these particular boys as family is definitely something worth being happy about.

"You coming?" Jamie asks me since I still stand two steps from the top where she left me.

"Yep," I say with a big smile. "Sure am."

As the Sunday afternoon moves on, so do the waves of laughter and manly gestures of strength. All the guys except Tate are gathered in the yard throwing rocks like shot-puts, smashing them into trees through the impenetrable forest beyond the yard, each competitor attempting to out-throw the other.

I watch from under the porch, sprawled out on the lounge chair with a blanket on my lap and a library book in hand, though the booms make it hard to concentrate. Tax is asleep, curled up under me.

Jamie is with Finn at the yard's far end, salivating over his gigantic muscular arms. He occasionally flexes, making her giggle, then she squeezes his biceps, swooning over him like a silly teenager.

"Pathetic, isn't it?" Tate says complacently, having

153

sat in the chair beside me undetected. "They've nothing better to do than show off to each other." He sneers.

Finding his judgment aggravating, I snarl. "They're bored. Guys do stupid stuff like that all the time. They're not hurting anyone."

"And what of the tortuous destruction they cause with every boulder they hurl? Does that not seem ostentatious to you? Intentionally spiteful even?"

His chastisement floods me with guilt, as if I am to blame by association alone. He speaks of the forest as a living being, feeling pain and suffering as we do. I know the woods to be their home, but I hadn't considered what they do as disrespectful or hurtful till now. Nonetheless, it is Tate's heartfelt loyalty to it that I find to be most surprising.

"Maybe they don't see it that way. You should point it out to them."

He huffs, "You think they'd listen? And I thought you were supposed to be smart," he adds, looking away.

"Excuse me? You don't even know me."

He huffs again. "Aren't you wolf chasers all alike? Hopeless romantics with a sick hunger for what could kill you?"

"Look, I didn't ask for this, remember?" I say, glaring at the back of his head. "Don't presume one is dumb because they look for simpler ways to resolve conflict."

"I see I've hit a sore spot. My apologies," he says over his shoulder. "I did not mean to offend."

"Yes, you did," I say bluntly, surprising myself. "But that's fine. I get that's how you are."

When he looks at me out of the corner of his eye, I see sadness there, but it disappears when he looks away again.

"I only thought it obvious that they loathe me. Why would they ever take my advice?"

Not knowing how to answer, I sit for a moment studying him.

"Why do you think that is?" I finally ask.

He shifts in his seat and says sharply, "I don't know, maybe because I've had 80-plus years of dealing with it. Why should I expect anything different?"

"But if you automatically assume it before they can prove you wrong, doesn't that make you prejudiced?"

The only reply I get is a huff and a shake of his

head like I'm being a clueless idiot again. It instantly aggravates me.

"Then again, maybe you enjoy wallowing in self-destructive isolation too much to do something about it—or so it would seem. What would be the point of making an effort at all if you've already given up, right? Or, is it the anticipation of the predictable letdown and the constant complaining about their hatred for you that thrills you too much to let go of, to actually try and make things better with them?" I swallow my nerve down hard, knowing I have jabbed at the figurative hornet's nest and have no idea what retaliation to expect.

He snorts. "Perhaps." Then he looks at me, his eyes rippling with anger. "But then again, what the hell do you know? You're just a stupid girl who's gotten yourself mixed up with something that will ultimately kill you!"

His words shock me. I want to retort, but I'm too appalled at his statement.

"You haven't the slightest idea what *my* life's been like. How I've been treated. You only see what they want you to see!" He growls, his nostrils flaring as if he'd just run a marathon. "But then again, I don't give

156

a damn about any of it anyway. I don't need them, and I sure as hell don't need you, so go ahead and keep your analytical prattle to yourself," he barks as he gets up and walks to the forest edge, where he disappears a moment later.

My hands are shaking; the adrenaline coursing through me is like an endless supply of caffeine.

My first instinct is to hate him on principle alone. But something inside me forces me to hesitate. Marcas had said Tate didn't get along with his brothers. Could some dark secret between them be driving Tate's anger and hatred?

Suddenly my intuition screams at me not to prejudge him, which goes against everything my brain tells me to do.

"Shae, you okay?" Jamie asks, walking up to me.

"Just thinking," I say as I continue to watch the spot where Tate entered the forest.

"Hey, so Sam and the guys want to go play some pool. You up for it?"

When I don't respond, Jamie touches my arm, lifting the haze in my brain.

"Wait, Sam wants to do what?" I say, looking at her.

Jamie shrugs, "Pool—in town. Since they're our bodyguards, we kind of have to go with them."

As concern tugs at me like a nagging toddler, I give Jamie a narrow look of warning.

"Come on, Shae, we've been cooped up here for days. Nothing will happen."

Being outside in a protected yard is deemed unsafe, yet venturing outside it is no big deal? Has everyone lost their minds?

"Jamie, I don't—"

"Did she say yes?" Finn asks, coming up behind her and putting his arm over her shoulder.

"No," she says, eyeing me as if trancing me into submission, "but she will."

Finn puckers up and smacks a kiss on her cheek. "Okay, but you better figure it out quick. Sam's chompin' to go." Then he runs up the stairs.

"Don't look at me like that!" I say, watching her eyelashes bat profusely, their magic of persuasion working overtime. "I'm serious, Jamie; no! Leaving—it's not a good idea!"

"Sam assured me Conall wouldn't dare show his face in town. Not after what happened with Marcas."

Part of me wonders if Sam would say just about

anything if it meant we'd agree to what we all know is the stupidest idea of all time.

With her hands together at her chest, Jamie begs, "Pleeeeeeese?" her face contorting like a sad old puppy.

Knowing if it wasn't for me, she wouldn't even be in this mess, I feel a wave of guilt. It cuts too profoundly to ignore.

"Okay, fine," I say, knowing I'd be outvoted at least four to one anyway. "But we're back by sunset."

"Thank you, thank you, *thank you!*" She grins and jumps on me, tackle-hugging me, making me crumble under her weight.

"Yeah, yeah, you owe me big!" I say, then eventually give in and laugh at her excited, goofy smile. "Now get off; you're squishing me," I add as I squirm under her.

"You call that squishing. I'll show you squishing." She rolls over and over, using the force of the turns to dig her hips and elbows into my body.

"Ough, your bony butt. Get off!" I yell and laugh in agony. She falls to the ground, landing on her side, laughing even harder.

"Girl-on-girl wrestling. Me likey," Sam cheers as

he and Ardan walk up to us.

While I help Jamie off the ground, we roll our narrowed eyes at him.

"So, ladies, are we doing this or what?" Sam asks.

Ardan's eyes shift to Jamie, a look of longing bright within them. Having seen that same lustful desire time and time again, I cringe; even among friends, she can't help but attract such attention.

"Yeah, give us a sec, would yuh?" Jamie says while straightening her disheveled hair.

"We leave in half an hour, with or without you being ready," Sam warns.

Jamie shoots him a look of confounded shock and then dashes for the stairs. Sam grabs her by the waist mid-step and pulls her back so he can go first. She huffs and tries to swipe at his ankle but misses.

Skipping two steps at a time, he yells, "Get a move on; we don't have all day," as he reaches the top stair.

"Sam, don't you dare go in that bathroom!" I hear her yell as she rushes into the house after him.

Ardan chuckles while staring up the stairs and says, "She's quite funny, very lively," as a smitten smile lingers on his face.

"That's Jamie for you," I say, reminding myself to

160

warn Jamie later about him. No good will come if this type of behavior continues. "Hey, nice job out there; you threw really far."

"Oh, you liked that, huh?" he says, bumptiously puffing out his chest. "It was nothing, really. You should see me in battle! I've taken out dozens of men with a boulder half that size and little else. No one gets by me!"

"Impressive," I add, suppressing my disgust.

When he gazes up the stairs again, I notice a flicker of something odd in his smile—mischievous and almost cunning. But as quickly as it shows, it is gone.

"Hey, where'd Niall go?" I ask, realizing I hadn't seen him pass us.

"To find Tate." He snarls. "You seemed upset earlier. What did he say to you?"

"Nothing, really, just being moody," I say, believing it best to keep our conversation a secret. "Is he always like that?"

"Don't trouble yourself about him. He basks in the joy of self-loathing, among other things," Ardan says flatly. "We should go inside. We'll be leaving soon."

I nod and follow Ardan up the stairs, the feeling of unease joining me. I can only hope nothing will go wrong while we're out.

CHAPTER 9

Never Say Never

As Sam had previously warned, in less than 20 minutes, we were packed into my and Jamie's cars and headed toward town.

On any other given summer day, Duke's is inhabited by hordes of twenty-something socialites with nothing better to do on vacation at the lake than to head into town and spend daddy's money. However, come on a leisurely late Sunday afternoon, and you might just think you've stumbled into a retirement community instead.

Case in point: several single, later-in-life women dressed in Sunday best sit at the table to the left of the bar, sipping pink cocktails with bright blue umbrellas tipped to the side—ordered specifically for Sundays. Not only do the ladies leave behind bright pink lipstick stains on the rims of their drink glasses, but also on their dentures as they smile. By which one is presently doing as she bats her eyes alluringly at two older gentlemen seated at the bar, dressed in faded three-piece suits with gray herringbone fedoras atop their heads. Her friend waves seductively in their direction as she sips her drink. Elvis Presley's *Don't Be Cruel* plays from the Jukebox by the bar and from the giant speakers overhead.

"Looks like it's geezer time at Duke's." Niall snickers while Sam and Finn rack up the ball on two of the four pool tables. When I snarl at him instead of smiling, he laughs again, shrugs, then moves to the table against the railing.

"Alright, let's do this! Amateurs take that table. Experts stay here," Sam says smugly as he and Ardan remain unmoved.

"You two against the girls? Alright." Finn shrugs while rubbing blue chalk on the end of his pool stick. "Niall, you good with that?"

"Yeah, either way," Niall affirms.

Sam and Ardan laugh robustly, leaning on their pool stick to keep from toppling.

"What, afraid we'll beat the pants off you?" Jamie snickers as she grabs a stick.

"Sh'yeah, right." Sam rolls his eyes. "Alright then,

rack 'em up. And don't think we're gonna go easy on you just because you're girls."

"What fun would that be?" I grin as I walk past him to get my own cue stick.

"He's good, you know," Niall says, leaning on the table to my right.

"Oh, I'm sure he thinks so," I mumble as I peruse the wall of sticks, then as I pick one, I turn and smirk at Niall like I know something he doesn't, which I do. "Jamie and I—Billiard Statewide champions two years running." I wink before turning around, my smile hidden. "We ready to start?"

"Bets anyone?" Niall calls while nodding subtlety as he passes. "I got a twenty here, says the girls take it all."

Sam and Ardan laugh even harder than before.

"It's your money," Sam says, slapping a twenty on the edge of the pool table. "Don't say we didn't warn you."

"Ladies first." Ardan beams mockingly, making way for us.

Jamie walks to the top of the table and pulls the bottom of her shirt down as she bends over, eyeing the table for the shot. While wiping her sweaty palms on the butt of her pants, she loses grip on the stick, which bangs down on the table. She cringes and gives a sheepish "Sorry."

Sniggering, the boys high-five each other with a

165

loud slap.

I give the boys a nervous side look as Jamie repositions the cue shaft, then gently glides it through her triangle-shaped fingers on the green velvet table.

Crack!

The shot scatters the balls around the table, placing three into separate pockets, all solids.

"I guess we call solids?" She says with a hint of a question as she leans her butt against the chair beside me. "Lucky shot, I guess." She beams, no longer hiding her joy.

Sam and Ardan exchange awkward glances, then silently bicker over who should follow the dominant break.

Losing, Ardan moves into position and motions with the tip of his stick. "Red stripe, corner pocket." Then he moves to strike. The balls bounce off the hole's edge, travel to the other end, and stop. He mumbles what I assume is a swear word as he shoves his pool cue at Ardan.

Jamie and I smirk. My turn.

"Last chance to call it a draw, boys. No sense in losing money if you don't have to," I say, lining up my shot. "We don't even have to call it if you don't want to."

"Will you just go already?" Sam says sharply.

"Suit yourself." I shrug. "Yellow, side pocket, and blue in the corner pocket." I pull back and shoot

166

without a second thought. The cue ball catapults forward, bounces off the walls twice at two locations, then strikes the balls, sending them precisely where I said they'd go.

Loud claps come from behind us.

"*Very* nice!" the shortest one of Conall's men says, examining the table.

"Tavis!" Sam snarls, leaping to my side in a flash, as does Finn to Jamie.

"Calm down, pup," Tavis says, raising his hand. The snake-like tattoo twisting around his wrist is like a bold declaration of his smug manhood, there for all to see. "I come waving my metaphoric white flag," he adds, as he bats his eyelashes, illuminating his ocean-blue eyes like a tractor beam.

Rogan and the young, skinny kid step forward, aligning with Tavis, their faces expressionless.

"Sure you do!" Sam retorts. "Like we trust anything you'd say."

"Where's Marcas?" Tavis asks coyly, looking among us.

"None of your business," Niall chimes in.

Tavis' eyes narrow. "Tate, Ardan." He nods. "Korin not around either? Meeting with Daddy, perhaps?" His words ooze out as his eyes linger on Ardan's face a second longer.

To my surprise, it is Tate, not Ardan, whose hands ball into tight fists like he's about to rip Tavis' head

167

off.

"I'll get to the point. Conall would like a word with the lady."

"Get the hell out of here!" Sam yells.

"Forget it!" Finn huffs.

"You've got to be kidding!" Niall agrees hurriedly.

"Come now, don't you want to end this?" Tavis counters. "Isn't that what you all want?"

"Yeah, right, like Conall would ever agree to that." Sam snarls. "You three can't be trusted, which goes double for him."

"You might be surprised," Tavis says with a hint of optimism.

Could it be that easy—talk with Conall and end this here and now? To do so scares me like nothing else, but if it's possible to change his mind, shouldn't I at least try?

Sam grunts, "Why don't you just take your little lackeys and get the h—"

I put my hand on his shoulder. "Is he really serious about ending this?" I say, looking hard at Tavis.

"What?" Sam stammers. "Of course, he's not!"

"Shae, no, it's a trap; can't you see that?" Jamie cries, her fear-filled, large eyes pleading with me not to do it.

Putting a hand on my shoulder, Tate turns me to face him. "You mustn't do this," he whispers in a rush.

"No good will come of it!"

His worry unnerves me. Is it even real?

Then I remember his glaring angry eyes from earlier, and I just don't know if I can believe it.

Clutching the necklace in my hand, I feel the warmth rise from it, almost unbearably hot, yet it does not burn me. Like a living, moving entity, my conviction grows; bravery and strength to fight for my future rise from the depths of me like a boiling teapot.

I know what I must do.

Giving a nod to Tate, I turn back to Tavis.

"I'll do it," I say quickly, moving forward.

Jamie screams, "No!" and Sam tries to grab me, but I am already beyond his grasp, Rogan stepping in to block him.

"Shae, stop! Think about what you are doing," Sam warns. Though anger is thick in his eyes, there is also fear. But I still do not heed it. He does not feel the electrifying feeling surging in me from the amulet. I don't know why it wants me to do this; I just know I must obey. It would never lead me astray, would it?

Staring at Sam firmly, I say with assurance, "I'll be alright." Then I turn to Tavis, who is smiling smugly, seemingly enjoying Sam's furry. "Stop smiling," I growl. "You three." I look from Tavis to Rogan and the other guy. "Leave. And let's be clear, I said I'd talk with Conall, but that's it."

"As you wish," Tavis says as he bows and points to

169

the circular wooden tables a foot from the stage, a single red rose in the glass vase in the center.

While the other two part the path to let me through, Sam lets out a monstrous growl and punches the pool table as I walk away.

Sitting at the table, I look for Tavis. As promised, he and the other two are nowhere to be seen. Looking at my friends, I see Sam standing rigid, arms folded against his chest, eyes smoldering in my direction, while everyone else watches me with worried stares.

Doubt chips at my certainty.

What have I done?

"You look even more beautiful than the last time I saw you," Conall declares with a smile as he sits across from me.

His happiness makes my stomach turn. "What do you want, Conall?"

"Come now, my sweet; you have better manners than that." He waves for the server. "Please, let me offer you a drink." A moment later, two glasses of a dark amber liquid are placed in front of us.

"I think we might have gotten off on the wrong foot," he continues, eyeing my untouched glass as he takes a sip from his. "I admit approaching you so menacingly that day in the woods was barbaric, but I had no idea you were the chosen one. Surely you can see my mistake was unintentional; we wolves have to eat, you know."

"You're serious," I huff. "That's your apology? You had to eat!"

His eyes hold a hint of shadowed annoyance, but his smile remains. "Though you doubt it, I mean every word, my lady."

"Trust you? The one who's been stalking me?" Even though my voice is strong, my hands shake in my lap. "Especially after Marcas told you to leave me alone!"

"I assure you; I have—"

"My cabin—broken into? You don't seem the type to let something like that happen without consent. So, was it on your orders, or done in defiance?"

"One cannot gauge just how far Tavis' loyalty will go. I'm afraid he acted out of anger. I reprimanded him as soon as I learned of his wrongdoings."

Conall's words sound soft and remorseful, but I refuse to trust them.

"He did say he had a tiff with your dog. No major wounds, I hope. You're lucky to have such a loyal companion."

"He's fine," I say, the blood in my veins boiling. "So, you've apologized. Does that mean you're leaving then?"

He gazes plainly at me as if I am but a statue, a piece of contemplative art to ponder.

"So, you were lying when you said you wanted peace?"

171

Again, there is no reply, only a slight smile on his crooked lips.

"Fine," I breathe out. "If you're not going to answer, then we're through here."

Conall suddenly laughs. "I love it! This—this newly-found sense of authority. Shae, finally, I dare say you will make a mighty queen someday."

My eyes narrow in on him. Does that mean he no longer wants me dead?

His smile broadens. "Oh, but make no mistake, I have spent a great deal of time debating your future—giving my options time to sink in." He winks. "However, I do believe that since I plan on being king, it is in my best interest to surround myself with people who bring great value to what I offer as ruler." He lifts his cup and takes a long drink before setting it back down gently on the table. "And my best chance for success will be with you by my side." He places his hand on mine and gives it a gentle squeeze.

Forcefully, I pull my hand free. "How dare you even—I could—would never—"

"I would think on it a moment, my dear."

"Stop saying that!" I glare. "I'm not your dear, sweetie, darling—anything! I'm with Marcas; you know that! I would never—leave him? —No!"

"Why is that, do you suppose?" he asks, his eyebrow pointed. "Because you trust him so much? He saves you, and what? You stay with him? Why?

172

'Obligation? Oh wait, let me guess, he told you in a heartfelt moment that you were his one love. That being parted from you would cause him unbearable pain?"

His twitter-pated expression sends my insides burning with rage.

"Do you think I'm stupid?" I say bitterly, trying to keep my voice from trembling and exposing my horror. "That I would fall for your lies? I know what you're doing, and if you think I'd leave him for you, you're severely misguided."

"I'm simply showing you an alternate explanation for his actions. Suppose he only fulfilled his role as human liaison when he saved you, per their law. Thou shalt do no harm; protect, defend, and whatnot." He rolls his eyes. "And at this point, he follows protocol, doing and saying all he can to seal the deal, if you will. You being the means to his rightful place as ruler. Maybe, just maybe, he carries on the facade long enough to obtain what he desires and will have no further use of you when he claims it.

No! Never. I know Marcas. He would never!

"Don't mistake him for being you," I say sharply. "He'd never do that to me. Your accusations are nothing more than the last desperate efforts of a cowardly, manipulative monster."

Conall pounds his fist on the table once, shaking the vase in the center.

173

Flinching, I hold my breath.

Patrons at the tables around us stare in disgust at Conall. He smiles nonchalantly at them, but his eyes burn with rage when he turns back to me.

"Do not mock me! I will not be trifled with. I'm not one of your lovesick puppies, yours to manipulate. I can end you here and now. Believe me, I could!" His eyes ripple with intense anger as his sharp words carry a heavy warning to my core. But then his eyes slowly soften as he sighs deeply and turns away, "But then that would hurt me. More than you know."

No! This isn't real. He has feelings for me? No-no, this is a game. It has to be!

"You're young and smart," he finally says, his voice light and gentle. "Though still naïve to believe your love is everlasting. You hardly know Marcas. Can you truly trust him with your life? Has he told you of his past? All his *secrets*?"

"Of course not, but that doesn't mean anything. I have secrets too. Marcas will tell me when he's ready."

"Don't be a fool!" Conall growls, looking sharply around to see if anyone heard him. "He doesn't tell you because he knows you will choose differently if you know the truth. Your love is feeble and hollow. I see it plainly on your bare hand." He pointed to the table, my hands hiding underneath it. "If he loves you, why deny you the one simple token of true love? I would not hesitate to let the entire world know that a

174

gorgeous creature such as yourself is all mine!"

Though Conall's confession sickens me, it also has a truth hidden within it. If Marcas knew we needed to marry, would he not have prepared for it?

No. I can't let Conall trick me. Time has been against us, and that's why we haven't—

"You're wrong!" I scowl. "Ring or no ring, Marcas said he loves me, and I believe him!"

"And yet I see the doubt in your eyes. Deep in your heart, you know there is truth in what I say." Conall pauses, observing me very closely, his eyes stern yet oddly warm. "We could be good together—the most powerful couple to rule, strong enough to take over and change everything."

"No!"

"Yes, Shae, open your mind to it. Free yourself of doubt."

"No!" I cry again, shaking my head profusely. "I don't doubt!"

"Oh, but you do." His smile widens. "See it for what it is, Shae, before it's too late! Come with me. Be with me!"

I want to scream at him with all my might how wrong he is, but my fear holds me back. Fear of making the wrong choice, fear that he could somehow be right about any of it. Fear of making any kind of decision at all. I just want this nightmare to end, for me to wake up and find this all a dream.

"Think on it," Conall says quietly. "Find me; I will be waiting."

When I look into his hope-filled eyes, my blood runs cold. He is nothing but manipulation and lies.

"Then you'll be waiting forever," I say, glaring as I stand up quickly.

Conall grabs my wrist hard.

Sam, Niall, and Tate are by my side in seconds.

"Let her go, Conall," Sam bellows with such authority that Marcas would be proud.

"Relax, pups, I merely wanted to pay my formal respects to the future queen," Conall says, staring knowingly into my eyes as he raises my trembling hand to his lips and kisses the back of it, then releases it.

Sam pulls me away with lightning speed toward the exit. Around tables and across the room, I follow without hesitation.

Outside the front door, the cars are waiting. Finn drives while Jamie sits in the back with me. Sam sits pensively in the passenger seat, glancing back at Ardan, Tate, and Niall, following closely behind in my car.

Except for the steady sound of the rough road under the tires, the quietness allows my brain to wander in its jumbled mess of knowledge and emotions as we drive. Conall's last words created an emotional upheaval I can't seem to shake.

Never did he want peace to end all this. He only wanted to see my face when he declared his intentions. I feel sick; a wave of guilt as epic as the stormiest of seas crashes over me.

What have I done?

Holding the necklace in my clutches, anger shifts inside me. I look down at it. Why? Why did it give me the strength to do what I must, only to have me fail? Why put me in danger for nothing?

No, not for nothing. Conall wants me alive and for himself. I know that now, though I desperately wish I didn't.

Without notice, we reached the house faster than expected.

Loud arguments erupt simultaneously when the door to the house slams shut behind the last person who entered.

With my legs pulled to my chest on my usual loveseat, I close my eyes and force back tears.

"You never should have let her go! Look at her; she's clearly upset." Jamie scolds Sam as if I'm not even in the room or capable of hearing what they say.

"Jamie, *back off!* Did she even give me a chance to stop her? No! So, shut up and let me think." Sam scowls.

"Don't talk to my girlfriend that way!" Finn says, getting in Sam's face. Ardan gets between the two of them before they have a chance to throw punches.

Then Jamie tugs Finn away from temptation.

"Guys, enough; this isn't helping!" Niall says, pacing back and forth in the kitchen, a loose floorboard squeaking with every other step he takes. "Someone just ask her what they talked about."

"Her speaking to Conall accomplished nothing, and he's obviously not backing down," Sam argues angrily.

"I'm sorry," I finally say, exhaling heavily as I look around the room. "I thought I could get Conall to change his mind."

"Shae, you need to tell us what he said," Sam says as he sits in the armchair next to me, his voice calm and collected once again. "We need to know, so we can protect you."

I shake my head slowly. "It's no use, Sam," I say, fighting back tears. "It won't change anything. Conall's mind's made up. He's coming, and nothing will stop him."

The unasked question of when drifts heavily in the room.

Humiliated and unwilling to let them see me cry, I stare out the window into the darkening night; the moon has not yet risen in the sky.

Sam puts his hand on mine and sighs. "Alright, it's getting late. Let's just . . . talk about it more tomorrow. Niall, you take the first watch, then Ardan," he adds, patting my hand before going to the

178

kitchen. Niall and Ardan agree to his order, and before they leave the room, I can hear them mumbling to one another in the far corner.

Pain hits my heart. I feel the fool. Even if the necklace made me believe I could handle myself, I knew better than to put myself in danger. Marcas—how can I face him?

Jamie slowly kneels beside me. "Shae, sweetie, let's get you in bed."

Her eyes, so full of worry, peer into mine. She wants me to tell her what bothers me, but I can't. I disgust myself for doing precisely what I had promised Marcas I wouldn't do—how I'd let Conall's theories about Marcas burrow doubt into me.

Like a prisoner to their cell, I follow Jamie to the bedroom and undress, then slip into my pajamas before climbing into bed without saying a word. She tucks me in, turns out the light, and closes the door until a crack of light shines at the foot of the bed.

Even though I try to block it out, I still hear muffled arguing coming down the hall. My stomach turns. What are they saying about me? That I'm such an idiot, that's what. How could I have ever thought speaking to Conall would get us anywhere?

Angry tears travel down my face and onto the pillow underneath my head as I clench my teeth. This is all Conall's fault. How dare he show his face and mess everything up. Hinting at having feelings for me;

what garbage! He doesn't know me or what Marcas and I have. Everyone can see he is nothing like Marcas and would never, even on his best day, compare to the king Marcas will be.

And yet, how little I know of their world is painfully apparent. It frustrates me how right Conall was. I am so utterly naïve and uneducated in their ways that I can't tell the difference between a lie and the truth.

Marcas—will he hate me for being so stupid?

CHAPTER 10

Heavy Is The Wait

The soles of my shoes slip on the damp grass beneath my feet, creating a loud squeak as they rub on the long blades of grass.

There is a coolness to the air, the sun's rays not quite reaching beyond the roof's threshold and into the yard; however, the chill is still not enough to force me back inside where everyone else remains. Their short-tempered, agitated selves, bickering at the slightest thing, only added to my self-contempt, knowing I was the cause.

Outside, I at least find some peace in my solidarity—a minuscule amount, but enough. If anything, moving about the yard keeps the crushing conflicting emotions and thoughts from wreaking havoc inside me.

Besides, even though it feels like it, I am never completely alone. Periodically, Sam and the others peek inconspicuously out the window at me. Knowing they aren't so mad they've stopped caring remains a comfort.

Even so, no harm will come to me out here. Conall confirmed it; he'd wait for me to go to him. The reality troubles me greatly, but it is also as if a weight has been temporarily lifted from me. Of course, he's a delusional psychopath to think he could persuade me to leave Marcas. But at least his belief in the idea bides us the time we otherwise wouldn't have.

"What are you doing out here?" Tate says, having come through the trees and into the yard.

"I could ask you the same thing."

"It's too dangerous; you shouldn't be out here alone." The sternness in his voice, as though scolding a misbehaving child, surprises me.

"I had to get out of there." I nod toward the house.

"Suppose anything's better than that." He snarls, then slowly turns towards the stairs.

"Tate."

He pauses, giving a side glance.

"Thank you—for having my back last night."

With a shrug, he huffs, "A lot of good it did."

"I know, but still."

182

Though his features remain stoic, the sting of his words had cut me. Why do I let him get to me? It's evident that, like Marcas when we first met, Tate runs hot and cold when the mood strikes him. A scowl here, a harsh word there, only to stand by my side when I need him the most. And now, he seems insulted that I didn't heed his warning. Why? It's not like I deliberately rejected his warning. The amulet's promptings had been too strong to deny. Nothing would have stopped me at that point, though now I would give anything to rid myself of this awful treacherous feeling.

"Did he hurt you?" Tate eventually asks, a look of concern flickering in his eyes.

"No, just the usual threat of utter peril and such," I say, smiling internally. For someone who thrives on not caring, Tate's oddly good at seeming like he does, as if he is losing grip on the wall suppressing his softer side deep inside him.

"You have a history with them, don't you?" I ask as a gust of wind sends a spiraling chill down my arms.

"Catch that, did ya?"

I shrug.

"Yeah, well, I'd bet everybody does these days with his delusions of taking over the world and all."

"What do you know of it?" I ask quicker than intended.

183

He glares, eyes dark and dangerous. "What, you think I have something to do with this?"

"No," I say calmly, though the sharpness of his tone makes me want to snap back at him. How can he expect anything but suspicion when he acts like that? "Just curious what you think of it."

His shoulders sink as he looks briefly up at the house, then back at me, "I know nothing of it, and that's the truth." His eyes narrow slightly. "No matter what others may say."

"But you must know something—what he's capable of."

He chuckles snarkily. "My brothers, discuss matters of the kingdom with me? You give me way too much credit. They trust me about as far as they can throw me." Then he snickers slightly, "And if you're wondering, according to Ardan, that'd be halfway across Montana."

"You sure?" I smile a little, believing the outlandish declaration possible. "With wind velocity, wouldn't it be more like all the way to Oregon?"

The corners of Tate's lips turn up slightly. "Or the coastline."

I laugh while his smile widens. For a moment, everything appears calm and peaceful. Even the wind seemed to stop. But then Tate's smile fades as a shadow shifts over his eyes.

"I'm not stupid, you know. I know what the others

184

have told you about me."

"They haven't-" The scowl he gives stops me from finishing. "So. I'm capable of coming to my own conclusions."

"You still think I care what you think of me?" he asks sharply.

Having felt the start of a connection with him, a heartache beats in my chest.

"You don't have to be a jerk, Tate, sheesh." I glare. "I was only trying to be friendly.

His eyes narrow. "You sure about that?"

"What, like *I* have ulterior motives?"

"As a matter of fact!" he scowls. "You want answers, and what, I'm your first choice? You should try to be less obvious next time."

"Is it so hard to believe that someone actually wants to talk with you," I snap, "to be nice to you without wanting something in return? Oh no, you can't risk the chance they may see the real you and actually care about you. Got to push them away. Wouldn't want to ruin your image. This whole *'everyone hates me'* Façade you have going; what a load of crap." I turn to walk away, but he snatches my arm.

"That's not who I am," he says hurriedly. "Not who I want to be." His sad eyes deepen. "I may not like my life, but I do care—believe me, I do. Though these days, it's harder to do."

Staring at his sorrowful eyes, lined with bitterness

185

and anger, I want to trust him, yet I remain unsure if I indeed can.

"Trusting people. I get it." I smile earnestly. "But not everyone is out to get you, Tate. I'm not—Marcas, either."

"I'm beginning to see that. Now." he smiles, causing the handsomeness of his heart to beam back at me. It's like looking into the eyes of a whole different person.

Giving a nod, I smile. "Good."

His wide grin lingered a moment longer before dropping into a hardened, stone-faced scowl once more. Giving a tight-lipped nod as if we are no more than unacquainted strangers, he then turns and walks up the stairs.

Just as he reaches halfway, Niall comes out and stands at the wooden railing, eyeing Tate as he walks past and into the house.

Did Tate know Niall was coming? Is that why he shifted so quickly?

Looking down at me, Niall smiles, though his happiness is overshadowed by his uneasy stance.

He waves awkwardly, and I smile back.

After bounding down the stairs, he skids to a stop before me. "Hey," he says with a slight grin. "What ya doin'?" Though his eyes remain fixed on me, they slightly shift as if wanting to return to the house, looking for Tate. "Everything ok? You've been out

186

here a while."

"Have I?" I say as I wander away from the house to a large stump in the furthest corner of the yard. The wood feels damp as I sit, but it's the least of my worries.

Niall remains standing.

"You know, you don't have to keep avoiding us. We're not upset."

"You sure about that?" I frown.

"Well, not anymore." He grins back. "You didn't give us much to go on last night."

"Sorry," I mumble, feeling the returning wave of regret and self-loathing wash over me. "I only wanted to make things better. To change Conall's mind," I say somberly. "That didn't happen."

"No," Niall huffs, his smile gone, "because when a shape-shifter turns his back on his clan, there's no going back. Nothing he says can be trusted."

My foolish heart aches as I nod away my loathsome feelings. How could I have been so stupid? To believe I could come even remotely close to fixing anything.

"What did he say?" Niall asks, shifting his feet.

Giving a slight shrug, I look down at my hands as thoughts bombard me. Not one of them do I wish to say aloud, for if I do, I can no longer deny their potential truth.

"Shae, you need to tell me."

"I know," I mumble, but I'm not ready.

Resting his hand on my shoulder, Niall sighs softly. "Please, Shae, let me be here for you." When I look up at him, his eyebrows furrow into a deep V. As his hand falls to his side, a rush of sorrow comes over me.

"He did most of the talking," I finally say, gulping down my self-disgust. "I sort of just sat there."

I want to say how scared I was, to confess I hadn't been as ready for it as I thought. But to admit that after insisting on my ability to handle myself, would be mortifying.

"He tried to convince me he didn't mean to try and kill me."

Niall grunts.

"And what happened at my cabin wasn't on his orders."

"Why am I not surprised? Deflect much?"

"He also said—" Unsure I can stomach saying it aloud, I squeeze my eyes shut briefly in hesitation and whisper, my voice slightly on edge, "—that . . . he wants me."

"Wait, like *wants you*, wants you?" Niall gasps.

I can't look at him to confirm it.

"Well crap," he says, more astounded than upset. "That just sucks buckets, now, doesn't it?"

"Now you believe him?" I say, looking at him sharply. "I thought you just said he lies and can't be trusted. Can't he be lying about this too?"

Niall frowns.

"Why not; if it gets him what he wants?" I say, heaving in breaths. I had been desperate for validation on how ludicrous this all sounds, but I never expected confirmation on its believability. Conall can't have feelings for me. He just can't!

"No!" I say, shaking my head fervently. "I've seen him twice, once when he almost killed me! Now he can't live without me? No—No! This is crazy—insane. No!"

"It'll be ok," Niall says, a hint of worry in his voice.

"Niall, I'm pretty sure a deranged, homicidal, lovesick guy with a heightened, uncharacteristic emotional state is extremely dangerous, especially in someone as warped as him! What part of that sounds okay to you?" I growl.

Niall moves to sit beside me. "It's true, this kind of passion, coming out of nowhere like-like lightning striking, is scary, but it can be dealt with."

"Lightening, really?" I say, rolling my eyes. "More like the Death Star suddenly destroying that one planet."

"Yes!" Niall laughs. Shifting off-kilter, he grabs my arm to avoid falling off the stump. "Nice reference!"

"I'm serious, Niall." I scowl, trying not to grin as I

pull him upright with my arm. "It's like stalker or killer; take your pick! And I'm not sure which one's worse."

"What if there's another explanation for his sudden change in heart?"

"How so?"

"The amulet. You know, the whole thing being a challenge for the future king and stuff. Fighting for love. That sort of thing. You can't fight if there isn't a—"

"Battle? Great," I groan.

"A challenger, at least. It wouldn't be the first time something like this has happened. My dad and his, remember? Once this is all over, Conall's feelings could dissipate."

"But his dad's never did! Conall's hatred is the exact product of that love triangle."

Once again, I find myself so completely lost in their world, having no idea if I will ever get a handle on any of it, that I feel my head begin to throb.

"Suppose what doesn't kill you—"

"Don't, finish that." I snarl, not liking how close to home it hits.

"Listen, it won't be easy, but we'll figure it out. Please don't beat yourself up about this."

"How can I not?" I say with weighted frustration, unable to dislodge the lump of guilt rising in my chest. "This is all my fault! And I can't stop it. I let him—" Feeling nauseated, I lower my head and hold my stomach as regret for what I've done, what I let happen, and what I've put everyone through, pounds deeper into my heart.

Niall softly puts a hand on my back. I want his comfort to make me feel better, but it only makes me feel worse.

"You let him what?" Niall says quietly. The strength in his voice makes me want to break down, but I am desperate to hold back the flood of tears, ready to break through my dam of shame.

"Conall, he." Taking a deep breath, I let it out slowly, my eyes still looking down. "He said Marcas is keeping things from me, things that would make me not want to be with him."

"That's a bunch of crap!" Niall snarls. "Like what?"

"He didn't say."

"Right, because there isn't anything!"

My heart is pounding, my body shaking. I don't want to speak of Marcas this way, but I am worried. Worried there could be truth to what I'm about to say next.

Swallowing down the bile I feel coming up, I whisper, "And that Marcas could be faking his feelings for me to get his crown." And I might just believe it. The thought rips at me like razor-sharp barbed wire.

"Damn it!" Niall suddenly growls, pounding his fist on his leg aggressively with such ferocity it makes me flinch. He stares hard at me with a storm of wrath in his eyes. It is like nothing I have ever seen on him before.

"I warned Marcas this could happen!" He breathes rapidly, his hands balled into tight fists. "But no, he wasted too much time, and now look what's happened!"

"Then it's true?" I say hysterically, on the verge of throwing up. "Marcas is using—" I can't even finish saying it. Fear for what this means and what I have gotten myself into by staying lodges in my chest; the pain is almost unbearable.

Niall's face, rigid with bitterness, softens. "Shae, of course not!" he says, grabbing my hands and squeezing. "It's just that you've been through so much, and Marcas wanted to give you time to adjust to things before—"

"Telling me the truth? Why? Because you think me a child? That I can't handle it?" I say sharply.

I am so sick of them keeping things from me—essentials, life-altering things—that I can't stop my anger at bay any longer.

"So far, nothing has been easy to hear. Not in the slightest, but that doesn't mean I don't want to know about it. What gives you the right to decide what I can and can't handle?"

"That's not it!" he says in a panic. "I wanted to; I did!"

"So, Marcas—" I scowl.

Niall's eyes narrow. "Don't forget who the bad guy is, Shae. Deception. Scheming to get what he wants. Those are Conall's tricks. He put this idea in your head."

"You all keep things from me." I glare, "about how bad things are. That's deceitful too!"

"That's not fair." He frowns. "We do it to protect you, not to trick you."

I know he's right, but their information filtering offends me too much to listen.

"Don't you see how this makes me feel? I don't know a damn thing about any of this, and you guys only tell me after I've already found out about it."

"I know, and I'm sorry. I wish there was a better reason than to protect you, but that's it."

Not liking the assumption that I need protection all the time like some fragile creature, I glare at him hard. "Why should I even believe any of you?"

"We would never lie about this. Never deceive you, Shae!"

"How am I supposed to know that?" I yell as tears stream down my face. Tears for my uncertainty, for fear of making the wrong choices. For not knowing who to trust. "That—all this—that Marcas' love for me is real?"

"Because we can't lie!" Niall bellows. As if said in an amphitheater, his words echo through the yard, followed by a stillness that settles in my bones. "Not about love," he adds softly.

Swallowing hard, I watch Niall's eyes shift from frustration to sadness.

"Our ability to love—it's so much more potent than anything else we experience. We do not speak of it lightly; we cannot lie about it or deny it even if we tried. If Marcas confessed it to you, then it must be."

As I sit silently, Niall watches me. Tears run down my face, but I do not move to wipe them away.

"Look, Marcas' done things in his past he's not proud of, things he can't change or take back, but not telling you about it isn't dishonesty; it's about timing. Are you always forthcoming with all your past issues?" He eyes me knowingly, and I feel my stomach lurch. He already knows I haven't been. Not until recently, that is.

"Shae, I know for a fact that none of his past choices would be so awful that you would leave him because of them. Please don't doubt Marcas!"

A cold sweat drifts over me as humiliation lingers. A bitter sob leaves my lips.

"Do you doubt him still?"

"No!" I sob, my nose stuffed to the point I can't breathe out of it.

Niall quickly grabs me and hugs me tight in the

194

most vigorous bear hug I think I've ever gotten. I almost can't breathe, but then again, I am also crying inexhaustibly.

Damn you, Jared, and damn these stupid trust issues you've left me with.

Taking a deep breath, I let it out hard and slowly pull away from Niall. "I mean it," I say, sounding nasally and unlike myself. "I don't believe Conall, Niall."

His kind eyes grow sadder as he looks into mine. "A part of you must if you're this upset about it."

I shake my head profusely. "No!" Feeling my throat tense again, on the verge of another hyperventilating crying fit, I clear it, but the discomfort remains.

"You just have to trust in what you and Marcas have. Trust us!" Niall says. "Conall would stoop to trickery and lies if he felt he was losing. To shift the distrust onto someone else. Classic move for him, by the way. He wants to convince you he's the one who's there for you. Not us. Can't you see that?"

"I do; it's just—" I squeeze my eyes shut.

Why? Why can't I just trust them? Trust that I am safe and right where I am supposed to be.

Looking down at my hand, I fidget with my ring finger, rubbing where a ring should be.

"He mentioned the ring, didn't he?" Niall says knowingly.

195

"You know." I sniff, still not looking at him. "It's kind of funny. I never even thought about it until he mentioned it." Looking at Niall, I try not to cry. "I'm not even ready for one. Maybe not for a while."

"But it still affected you, what he said, didn't it?" Niall gives a soft understanding smile, his eyes shadowed with tenderness and worry.

I nod again and wipe a tear from my chin.

To be upset over something I don't even want right now seems mental, but then again, I am an emotional wreck, so why not roll with it?

"There's so much you don't know about us—our traditions, our culture. And because of Conall's meddling, we haven't had a chance to discuss any of it. He knows this and uses your lack of knowledge to make you think Marcas doesn't love you enough. Believe me when I say that Marcas *loves* you!" Niall stares hard at me as if to burrow his words deep into me. "And it has nothing to do with a crown. I would know! Losing you would destroy him."

I've been so stupid—blind to fall for Conall and his doubts. I knew he couldn't be trusted the moment I heard his voice in the shop that day. I knew it when I met him at the rodeo. Yet somehow, I let him put doubt into everything I knew to be real.

A sputter of shame shifts in my chest, but I hold it in.

"You okay now?" Niall asked after letting me sit

196

in silence for a while.

Looking at him, I am greeted with a soft, pleasant smile, as if he means to take away any residual sorrow I may feel.

I smile back through my tears and shrug. "Thanks, Niall, for being here for me."

"Eh, what's a future brother-in-law for?" He smiles, nudging his shoulder into mine.

The quietness of the yard soon takes over. Niall sits as still as I am, like we are two gnomes in a garden of evergreens. Yet an underlying nagging feeling keeps at me, forbidding me from enjoying it completely.

"Niall." I let out a heavy sigh. "What will my life be like if everything works out as planned?"

"Hard to say. Marcas' the first of his generation to take over."

"But don't they teach you about this stuff? Royalty family and all?"

"Yeah, but I'm not the important one." Niall laughs, but then seeing my angst, he shakes his head. "It's ok, though; we still have a purpose. My brothers and I are Marcas' right-hand men, fighting alongside him until our last breath."

"You're entire lives? Don't you get a future of your own?"

"We can marry; have families if that's what you mean. But we are also warriors, bound to him by

197

blood. You know, follow him around, doing his laundry, massaging his feet, feeding him grapes—that sort of thing," he says realistically.

"Really?" I ask, astonished.

He nudges my arm. "Sheesh, you're gullible.

"Nice, Niall, I'm trying to have a serious conversation here," I say, pretending to slug his arm.

He laughs. "And I'm trying to lighten you up." He shakes me back playfully. "Besides, the warrior for life part is true."

"That doesn't sound fair."

He shrugs. "Don't misunderstand; I want to protect him. It's an honor."

"So, you're saying if I were to have children, my firstborn would eventually take Marcas' place? And the others, his warriors?"

"Yeah, but that part never bothered me. My loyalty to Marcas is genuine, so it's ok."

"Is that the same for all clans?"

"Treason among siblings can happen, but it's rare. But not us. We truly care about what happens in each other's lives."

"I see that."

"Do you also see now why we're so excited about you and Marcas?"

"But look at all that's happened!"

"What, Conall? Pshaw, we already figured he would try and pull something. Besides, you forget all the good you've done. Take me; you befriended me and saved my nerdy hide multiple times even after I pushed you down, made you cry, and put you in awkward social situations."

"You're hardly a charity case," I say heartedly.

"No, but your friendship means more to me than anything, and nothing you could do would change that. Nothing."

"Ah, Niall," I say, trying not to get teary-eyed. "You're going to make me cry."

He grins, "And don't you even get me started on how much you've changed, Marcas. I hardly recognize the old softy."

Knowing soft isn't the word I'd use, I smirk. "How was Marcas before?" To say I am curious is an understatement.

"Negative. Overbearing. Kind of what you've already seen." He chuckles to himself. "But now, well, besides being borderline obsessively protective, he's more empathetic. Anyone can see you make him a better person." Niall shifts his butt on the stump and glances around the yard. "Of course, he'd still definitely kill me if he ever knew I told you that!"

I can't help but grin at his cowardice. "So, what made him such a—"

"Hard-ass?" Niall points his brow. "You remember me mentioning our sister, Vevina, right?"

I nod, my ears perking up. I knew there had been

199

more to the story than they led on.

"Well, they had been inseparable. Closer than any siblings I'd ever known. He once said she was the best of us, destined to do great things." Niall then frowns, a slight glistening in his eye.

I swallow hard. This can't be good.

"One day," he continues, a heaviness to his tone, "they had gone on one of their usual walks in the woods—in human form, that is." He smiles, though I can still see the heartache hidden there. "Hours later, Marcas stumbled back to camp alone, barely making it before losing consciousness. Later he couldn't recall how he'd gotten there, let alone where Vevina was."

Goosebumps travel down my arms like electricity while my heart pounds in my throat. Poor Marcas!

"Our father went ballistic when he found out, searching everywhere, but there was no sign of her, not a single clue. She had just vanished."

"How awful," I gasp, feeling a tweak of ache in my chest so much that I hold my breath to make it stop. "I can't imagine living through something like that."

Niall nods his head and gives me a knowing look. "To this day, no one knows what actually happened. Marcas tried for years to remember, but he never could. Not a single memory of any of it. And it tortured him.

'From then on, things were different. He didn't laugh. Didn't allow himself any ounce of enjoyment.

He became all consumed with rules, insistent upon never losing focus on the task at all costs.

'I know he blames himself for what happened to her. We tried to convince him he wasn't at fault, but he could never let it go."

"That explains why he's so protective of me," I say quietly. "Did your father ever forgive him?"

Niall looks at me, his eyes glistening. "Father knew the second she disappeared who was to blame, but there was no convincing Marcas to forgive himself for what happened, and it almost ripped our family apart."

"Conall," I whisper. The sharp pain of shame squeezes my heart to the point of agony. Meeting with him had been more of a mistake than I could have ever realized.

"Hey," Sam yells down to us from the top of the stairs, making Niall and I jump. "Marcas called. They're almost here. He wants us all inside." Then he walks back into the house.

My pulse quickens. From fear or eagerness, I'm not quite sure.

"I think you should tell Marcas about last night."

"What? No! I can't!"

"If it were me, I'd want to know. Marcas needs to tell you everything else so Conall can't fill your head with believable lies," he says firmly.

"I can't tell him that I saw Conall—talked with

201

him—believed his—"

"Marcas will understand."

"But so many things could have gone wrong!"

"But they didn't."

Blowing out a hard breath, I snarl. "Yeah, well, we're dang lucky."

"Luck or not—no going back now."

Niall stands up, steps toward the house, then turns back around. "You coming with?"

"I-I can't do this!" I shake my head.

"I'll be there with you. It'll be alright. I promise!"

I give Niall a hard stare down, not believing for a second he would ever stand up against Marcas at any moment in this lifetime—well, I guess other than the one time at Duke's—but that was because the pain he saw in me was raw, real, and happening right in front of him. This time he has too much time to chicken out.

"Listen—sure, he'll be upset, but I know him. He'll forgive you; trust me. You acted out of our best interest. He can't stay mad at you for that, can he?"

"One can hope," I say as Niall grabs my hand and helps me up. He shoots me an *at-a-girl* smile, puts his arm around my shoulder, and pulls me along.

I smile back half-heartedly. "Where would I even begin?"

"Tell them what Conall said."

As I rest my head against his shoulder while we

202

walk, he puts his jaw against the top of my head and adds, "And when that's over with, take a shower because you look awful." He leaves a hint of a smile in his tone. I shove him away, a small smile peeking through my troubled features. "I'm kidding." He pulls me close again and laughs as we reach the bottom steps. "Only a tiny bit awful."

CHAPTER 11

Repercussions

Even in a crowded room among friends, I feel so alone.

Everyone is scattered to all corners of the room. Niall sits in the armchair while Jamie, Finn, and I are on the long couch. They remain motionless, tense, and unbelievably close to one another on the opposite end, as if I have an illness they are afraid of catching.

Sam, at the kitchen table, taps his foot to the beat of the clock while gnawing on a piece of jerky, like an impatient beast, ripping and viciously tearing pieces off as he glares at a spot on the rug. The potent hickory and black pepper aroma permeate the room with every bite.

Ardan and Tate join us just as the door at the other end of the house opens and closes with a bang.

Sputters of elation momentarily overshadow my guilt and feelings of trepidation.

"Good, you're all here." Marcas glances my way, a smile of bewilderment on his face. I smile back, happy to see him even though my palms begin to sweat as unease leaps up and takes hold.

Joining Ardan on the loveseat, Korin sits on the armrest, their enormous muscular bodies too big to sit side by side.

Marcas remains in the center of the room, arms folded against his chest.

"So, how did things go here?" he asks plainly. "Anything to report?"

No one makes a sound, no eye contact with another.

"Nothing?" he asks, shifting to face his brothers. "Sam? Finn? Not a thing to mention?" When they don't respond, Marcas eyes narrow. "Well, that's odd because that's not what I heard!" he says sharply. "Imagine my surprise when one of Tynan's men told me you had left the property—defied my orders and left!" he yells loudly, yet I think Jamie and I are the only ones to jerk.

"Actually," Sam begins but stops short by Marcas' piercing glare.

"Seriously, Sam, if I'd thought you'd do something that stupid, I'd have—" He doesn't finish his thought, though it's obvious what he's thinking. And there's no way he could not have gone. It was too important. "Damn it," he growls and starts pacing back and forth.

"If I may, Marcas," Ardan says with conviction while standing. "We figured since we were in a public place and all together, we could keep the girls safe."

Marcas' head jerks sharply toward Ardan, his anger stabbing through him like a knife.

"Ardan, mind your place!" Korin growls. "You bring dishonor to Father by disobeying Marcas' orders."

Ardan sits back down with a heavy umph.

"Technically, we didn't disobey," Tate mumbles from a seat in the corner as he watches an insect scurrying across the carpet. "You never said stay *here*; only ordered them to be kept safe. As you can see, no harm came to them; we did our duty."

206

I am only a duty to him now? How can he sit there and say such hollow things, dismissing the worry and concerns I know were there before, as if the incident was nothing?

"You use a technicality to defend your idiocy?" Korin snarls. "I thought you smarter than that. You're lucky nothing happened because it would have if Conall wanted it to!"

A tingle of dread travels up my neck as I recall Conall's face when he told me not to mess with him and the terrifying strength he obviously had held back for my sake.

"Look, we didn't know Conall was just going to show up like that," Sam says hurriedly, as if one could even defend the idea of the inevitable being a slim chance.

"What the hell do you mean Conall was there?" Marcas growls, fury running wild in his eyes.

Flashes of hot and then cold rush over my body. Marcas didn't know!

"I can't believe—do you not see the danger you put her in? What could have happened to her?" He yells, pointing to me but directing the brunt of his wrath at Sam, then moves down the line, stopping at

207

Niall.

The pitiful, gut-tugging turmoil I see in Niall's eyes hurts my heart.

Knowing I had put myself in danger, not them, I force down the bile I feel rising in my throat as I stand up slowly, trying not to shake.

"I'm the one who agreed to speak with Conall. They tried to stop me, but I wouldn't listen. I only wanted—"

"You—spoke with Conall?" Marcas spits the words out like a bitter drink. "You let her go near him?" His green eyes, so big and so full of heated rage, dart from one brother to the next.

"Please, Marcas, let me explain," I plead, stepping toward him, my hand outstretched. He quickly pulls away from me, every muscle in his body tense, his eyes frenzied with outrage and a hint of disgust.

A cold jolt of pain floods my heart, stopping me where I stand.

My hand falls to my side.

Just like before, Marcas' rejection stings right to my core. The difference is, this time, I know I wholeheartedly deserve it.

Unable to stomach it happening in front of

208

everyone, I rush past Marcas and into the cool late afternoon air, the door slamming hard behind me. Loud arguments immediately commence back inside.

Running down the stairs, I nearly trip, missing the last step. It takes everything in me not to keep running and escape further humiliation.

Wrapping my arms around my chest, I start pacing the lawn. Back and forth, I move, my breath rapid, my mind racing.

I don't blame Marcas. I can't! He has every right to be angry. I betrayed his trust; I chose to put myself in danger. This time, I hurt him, and it pains me to the point of tears to see his eyes mirroring the same disappointment I have in myself for what I've done.

The chill in the air quickly seeps into my bones despite the heat rising from me as I keep moving.

The yelling inside continues for a while, yet no one else joins me. Sometimes I hear Marcas above all others. Other times I hear Sam fight back.

What have I done?

Eventually, the noise diminishes to nothing but silence. By then, my energy had depleted to nothing once the initial adrenalin had worn off. I now sit on the lounge chair, waiting for what is to come.

Slowly, Jamie comes down the stairs, one long, heavy step at a time.

"Hey," she says, reaching the bottom step. "You've been out here a while. You should come inside."

"No, thanks, I'm good." I stare blankly into the late evening sky. Dark gray clouds paint the edges of the horizon, as the rest of the sky is surprisingly blue and clear. Thousands of stars will be out once the sun goes down.

Clutching her arms, shivering, Jamie takes a step closer.

"Want me to hate him again for you?"

I grin and shake my head. "No."

"You made a mistake," she says, sitting on the chair beside me. "That doesn't mean you deserve to be outcasted."

"I'm not. Marcas just needs time to cool off." I shrug, trying not to show how much his actions hurt me. "Considering I broke a promise, I think he handled it pretty well," I add, staring into the fading evening. "Sorry about last night. I didn't mean to do that to you guys. I was only trying to help."

"We know. Niall sort of explained a few things after you left."

"Figured as much. How did Marcas take it?"

"He yelled loudly, a lot. Said the guys should have never taken us to Duke's in the first place, then yelled some more about honor and duty. I don't know; I tried not to listen after that. I wanted to leave, but I had to support Finn, you know."

Looking at her, I smile warmly. "As you should have."

"Niall told us what you and Conall talked about. As I'm sure you heard, Marcas lost it."

"I was afraid of that. Are the boys ok?"

"Eventually, but they had to have seen it coming." She reaches over, wraps her arms around me, and rests her head on my shoulder. "And I'm sure you're right about Marcas needing time."

Releasing me, she sits up and looks at me, her brow creased. "Marge called. She wanted to make sure I'm planning on coming in tomorrow."

"No, it's too dangerous!"

"Shae, I've already called in once. I have to go; she needs my help."

"But what if something goes wrong?"

"Shae, I'm nobody. You're who Conall wants. Besides, Ardan offered to stand watch." She smiles,

211

but the corners of her lips don't quite reach as far as they should. "I'll be fine."

"Why can't Finn go with you?"

"Can't. Marcas needs him. They need to talk about strategy or something like that. Besides, you worry too much."

"And you, not enough! Jamie, Ardan—he's not—he can't watch you."

"Why not?"

"Jamie, seriously, have you not seen him watching you all the time? That look he gives?"

"He's harmless. A little crush. It's not like it hasn't happened before."

"The last thing we need is him daydreaming about you, and something awful happens."

"Don't be—" Jamie stops, having noticed something behind me. A large, crooked smile spreads over her face, and she points over my shoulder with her eyes.

I don't have to see him to know who it is, but I look anyway.

Marcas is standing at the edge of the stairs, kicking at a large clump of dried mud caked on the side of the post. His eyes dart up, watching us cautiously, obviously wanting to talk but also not wanting to interrupt.

"Let's talk more later." Jamie hugs me again.

Marcas mumbles, "Hey," as she skips past him and up the stairs. He looks so unbelievably sexy with his hands shoved deep into the pockets of his jeans. I can't help but smile. If he was mad before, he doesn't look it now.

Slowly, we walk toward each other. Taking his hands from his pockets, he wraps his warm, inviting arms around me and puts his forehead to mine. For a long moment, we allow ourselves time to hold one another in blissful silence, inhaling steadily in unison as though we are one.

He breathes out deeply. "I'm an idiot," he finally whispers.

"No," I say softly, squeezing him tighter, having missed him more than I'd realized. "You were upset and worried."

"I hurt you again, and I promised I wouldn't."

His struggle between justified anger and an impossible promise fills me with hope. To think he could keep heartache, pain, and unpleasantness from me for a lifetime is impractical but also very sweet.

That kind of love and devotion to one's happiness is hard to come by.

Moving my face to look up at him, I see a giant frown on his lips as his dark green eyes flicker with sadness in the twilight.

"You know, you're not supposed to apologize when I do something wrong," I say with a hint of teasing.

"Niall told us everything." He caresses my cheek, and it feels so inviting that I hold my breath, wanting to retain the warmth of his touch. "I was upset before, but I understand now."

Eventually, I exhale, knowing it's never easy to admit stupidity. "I'm sorry, Marcas." My voice quivers as I hold back tears of regret and disgrace. "I was so stupid! I should have never—"

"Shhh, Mo Chroi, it's ok, we'll stop him, and everything will be fine."

"But he wants me!"

Marca's jaw clenches, forming hard bumps at the back of his jawline. "I'm definitely *not* thrilled to know that, but also not surprised. Outside of making him king, you're beautiful, brave, strong-willed, compassionate—everything a man could ever want."

Shadowed by guilt, the compliments cut rather than thrill me.

I look down. "Marcas, I would never—"

Bringing my chin up, he kisses me softly, then stares deeply into my eyes. "No matter how hard he tries, he will never come between us."

Studying my face, he gently moves a strand of hair from my forehead and tucks it behind my ear. Taking a sputtered deep breath, he puts his hand in mine before exhaling deeply.

"Shae, you deserve better than this; better circumstances, better location, better everything."

Hearing him say my name sends shutters of curiosity up my spine.

"Forgive me for all of it; I beg you."

"Marcas, there's nothing to forgive."

He nods and looks down. "But there is. In the middle of a battle for a crown, I fell in love with you. With that love came great risk—sacrifice—a destiny you knew nothing about nor chose for yourself. Shae, I love you. And I want nothing more than for you to love me. Not my crown, not the life as a wolf that comes with it, just me."

Lifting his other hand, Marcas reveals a small

burgundy wooden box with identical carvings on the lid that match the amulet around my neck.

I gasp and squeeze his hand tight to keep mine from shaking.

He smiles, his eyes sparkling. "What I feel here," he says, moving my hand to his chest, where I feel his heart sputtering as wildly as mine, "is something so intense, natural, and real, like nothing I have ever felt. And I'll be damned if anything but true love could cause such a fierce feeling.

'I know this seems fast, but I also know you and I belong together. I've known it from the moment I first saw you."

Staring into his magnificent green eyes, I am beside myself. To hear such words from the man I love overwhelms me to the point of utter joy.

"Will you do me the honor of being my wife and my queen?" He opens the box, revealing a large princess-shaped diamond resting in a bed of fiery red gemstones shaped like a star with little, shimmering diamonds encircling it.

"Oh—wow, that's gorgeous—so big." I stammer breathlessly, my heart pounding in my chest.

Grinning, he holds my trembling hand steady

216

while getting the ring from the box and putting it on my finger. It slides on as effortlessly as a glass slipper, a perfect fit.

"Nothing would make me happier," he whispers, watching me intently.

Shaking slightly on my hand, the diamonds reflect the light above us, casting iridescent star shapes all around.

His wife. His queen. Am I really ready? So much change all at once. I-I can't think.

Moments feel like hours.

Looking down at the massive chunk of rock resting on my finger, I bask in its dazzling perfection. If ever there was a ring to choose from, if price nor circumstance restricted my options, this would be the one, above all others.

Breathe, Shae. Think. He loves you—yes, most definitely. He can provide, protect, and make you happy—again, yes, in every way possible! And you love him? Unequivocally! Then what are you waiting for?

I smile at him as excitement rushes me like a freight train through my whole body. This feels right. Feels organic. Feels like home. This choice—my choice. My future to pick . . . and I choose—"Yes!" I nod happily.

As I throw my arms around Marcas' neck, he lifts me, and I kiss him. Every ounce of love, affection, devotion, and desire flows through every kiss, so he will know *I* choose him, now and always.

"I love you," I whisper in his ear.

"And I, you, Mo Chroi." He squeezes me tight and then kisses me again.

Within the forest beyond the yard, thunderous, agonizingly torturous sounding howls echo off the mountainsides; so loud and full of agony, one would believe death would soon follow whatever beast had made it.

But I don't have to guess, recognizing it the moment it reached my ears.

Pulling away from Marcas, I gasp, "Conall!"

CHAPTER 12

It Isn't So.

The hairs on the back of my neck stand on end. My knees buckle from under me, and I cling to Marcas like I'm on the edge of a cliff about to fall to my death.

Coming from inside the house, I hear Tax's distant howling echoing the ones coming from the forest.

Everyone but Jamie and Korin leap down the stairs just as the eerie sounds cease.

"Dude, what was that?" Sam asks as he skids to a stop under the porch where we stand.

"Conall," Marcas states while helping me steady myself. "Take the boys and make sure he leaves the area. We don't want him to circle back and attack without warning."

"On it," Sam says as Finn, Niall, Ardan, and Tate race across the yard with him. In mid-stride, they reach the boundary and transform before my eyes. Seeming smooth and effortless, hands and legs morph into paws as a furry tail extends from their backsides. Each step they take makes their features more wolf and less human. Just as their bodies shrink until their true forms manifest, they sprint out of the yard and into the night.

"Did you—just see—wha—" I mumble.

Marcas grins sheepishly. "Come on, let's get you inside." He takes my hand in his as I reluctantly follow, still trying to see behind me.

Jamie is frozen at the top of the stairs, her pale face visible despite the lack of good lighting.

"Jamie, hey, you all right?" I ask, skipping up the stairs to reach her, but she can only slightly move her head in reply. "What's wrong with her?"

Marcas moves around us and opens the front door. "A bit overwhelmed by what she saw, I think."

"Come on, sweets," I say as I wrap my arm around her and lead her into the house, then over to the couch next to the window, where she proceeds to sit, staring blankly into the yard.

"Place it on her neck; it'll help," Korin says, handing me a damp towel. With a trembling hand, I take it and thank him before doing as suggested.

"I can't believe that just happened." I say, taking a deep breath, the adrenaline still pumping, making my heart pound like crazy. "It was amazing!"

"Isn't it? Like an interpretive dance," Korin adds, handing Marcas and me a piece of red licorice.

"It'll help with the shakes," Marcas says, smirking.

"Stop smiling; it's not funny," I growl, smacking his chest with the back of my hand. "I wasn't expecting them to just change like that. You could have warned me or something."

"But I thought you'd already seen it."

"Of course not. When would I have?"

"I assumed, Niall, when he met you at the park that one day."

My jaw practically drops to the floor. "That was—that punk—he nearly scared me to death. What was he doing sneaking around in there?"

"I sent him to watch over you," Marcas says matter-of-factly, his smile still evident in his eyes.

"Oh! I guess it's okay then." I shrug, blushing.

While holding the towel to Jamie's neck, I stare out the window as worry for my friends moves to center stage.

"Will they be okay?" Jamie finally asks, still watching the yard. She takes the towel from me and puts it on the windowsill.

"I believe so," Korin says, still sounding unsure.

His uncertainty frightens me.

"Conall's wounded, to be sure," Marcas says, hugging me from behind as I take Jamie's hand, "but there's no way of knowing how he'll react. We've underestimated his response once before. Best to not do it again."

"Sam won't attack if they find him, will they?" I ask, gulping down my worst fear. "I don't want anyone getting hurt!"

Marcas squeezes me gently. "They'll be fine. They know what they are doing."

"Wha-what if it's a trap?" Jamie stammers. "Luring them out there to—"

"Conall won't be looking for a fight. Not now. Not after Shae made her choice," Marcas relays as he looks at me. I still see the worry in his soft eyes.

I feel a shift inside me. This is my fault. Once again, I have done something to tip the balance, to make things even harder than they need to be. I don't regret saying yes to Marcas, but the timing—why did Conall have to see it?

"But he could still fight back if threatened—hurt someone!" Jamie says, forcing back tears of worry.

"She's right." Korin shoots Marcas a quick glance. "You know as well as I do, wolves love more profoundly than humans. Whether the amulet's pull makes him feel this way or something deeper, it doesn't matter; pain is pain, and by the sounds of it, he's in a lot of it."

222

"Call them back," Jamie says sternly. "Now, before—"

"Look!" Korin cries, pointing out the window.

A human figure staggers onto the grass at the edge of the trees. Exposed to the moon's light, the shadowy being steps and then falls to the ground.

Jamie and I both scream.

Marcas races from the house and down to the motionless body.

Jamie clutches my hand tight, and as fear grips us completely, Jamie chants, *'Please don't let it be Finn'* over and over under her breath. I beg for it, too.

Without effort, Marcas lifts the person to his feet, hoists their limp body over his shoulder, and then races back up the stairs and into the house. I drop Jamie's hand and dart for the door.

When Marcas enters, I gasp in horror. "No-no, no, not Niall!"

"Shae, open his bedroom door, please," Marcas orders calmly as he shifts the weight of his brother's body on his shoulder.

"Please be ok, Niall. Please," I sob as Marcas lays Niall gently on the bed. Almost immediately, Niall begins to stir, moaning in pain as he moves.

"Oh, thank goodness!" I cry as I kneel on the floor by his side.

Niall continues to moan and wriggle about while Marcas removes Niall's shoes and then searches him for blood, broken bones, or any other obvious sign of injury.

"Marcas, what's wrong with him?" I say, panic-stricken.

"Nothing. No blood. Not a scratch."

"Niall, please, tell us what's wrong!" I beg.

Niall moans loudly into the mattress.

"Marcas, I can't—"

Moving to switch with me, Marcas then leans in close to Niall. "Niall?" he whispers. "Where are you hurt?"

Between the muffled wails and painful growls, Niall manages to whisper something back. Jumbled up and incoherent, I can't make it out.

A grin forms on Marcas' face. "That's what I thought." Then he stands.

"Thought what? Marcas, tell me!"

Grabbing my hand, Marcas sighs, "Let's give him time to rest," and gently tugs me along toward the door.

"Wait, Marcas, I can't just leave."

"Don't worry; he'll be alright."

"But I need to—"

Marcas squeezes my hand affectionately as he closes the door behind us. "I'll check on him in a while, just in case."

Even though I glare in protest at him, I let him guide me back to the living room.

"What's the damage?" Korin asks, concern resonating in his tone.

"He looks like death!" I exclaim, "But Marcas doesn't seem to think it's *that* bad!" Then I glare at him again just in case he doesn't understand how upset I am.

Marcas' smile broadens, causing Korin to counter with one of his own.

As I am now glaring at them both, Korin laughs.

"You better tell her before you wind up sleeping on the floor tonight." He grins, nudging his head in my direction. "Because I won't give up my couch for nothin'!"

Marcas draws me close, lightly snickering. "He'll be just fine, Mo Chroi."

"He's at death's door in there, and you think it's nothing?" I huff, trying to wiggle free from his arms to get back to Niall's bedside.

"Alright, Shae, stop, okay, I'll tell you." Marcas forces his smile away. "Niall told you about the final change, right?" I nod and open my mouth to speak, but Marcas shakes his head. "Then you know, even though it hurts like hell, he'll be fine."

"Change." I breathe. "You're sure?"

Seeing my worry, his eyebrows furrow. "I promise. It looks a lot worse than it is." He then leans in and kisses my forehead, then my nose, before finally placing a soft, sweet kiss on my lips. "I love how big

225

your heart is. He'll be glad to hear you care so much. He thinks of you like a sister, you know?"

"Yeah, I know," I concede, "And like a sister, when he gets better, I'll kill him for putting me through this."

Marcas and Korin both laugh.

*　　*　　*

The frigid wooden floor stings my bare feet as I tiptoe down the darkened hallway.

Slowly and quietly, I open the door to Niall's room, cringing as it lets out a slight squeak when it closes.

Niall's body, shadowed by the room's darkness, lay in a large mound across the bed, arms and legs sprawled out in all directions. He snorts and rolls onto his side.

Relief washes over me; the worst is over.

When he doesn't move again, I slowly turn and reach for the doorknob.

Suddenly a hand reaches around and presses over my mouth, making my heart leap into my throat.

"Don't scream," says a deep, raspy voice in my ear. "I'll take my hand away if you promise not to go crazy on me and wake everyone up."

Frozen, I give a slight nod, and he does as promised.

"Who . . . are you?" I whisper, squinting at the towering figure in front of me.

"It's my room. Who else would it be?" he chuckles quietly.

"Niall!" I gasp, watching the massive silhouette of his body blend into the darkness as he moves back to the bed and sits down. When the table lamp flicks on and the room comes into view, I finally see him, no longer the scrawny boy I once knew.

Stumbling back in surprise, I bash my elbow on the corner of the dresser, knocking several items to the ground. Though a sharp pain throbs from my arm, I remain motionless, fixated on the stranger before me like an animal desperate to remain unseen by a predator.

Niall smiles, and in a flash, I see him still in there. Though now more of a younger version of Marcas, his nose, cheekbones, and chin are undeniably Niall's—a more chiseled, defined, and masculine set of features, but his nonetheless. His hair, now completely black, has cowlicks all about his head, while his green eyes mimic the sinister look I recognize all too well.

He is the spitting image of the drawing I made of him, as if I had drawn it from memory, not my imagination.

Slowly, I crouch for the fallen object and quietly put them back on the dresser, my sight not once leaving Niall.

"It's alright, you can say it." He looks at me with a cocky smile. "I believe brutally handsome were the words you were looking for."

With my eyebrow peaked, I smirk. "You'd like me to say that, wouldn't you?"

"Eh, wouldn't hurt for you to admit it."

"Keep dreaming."

Transfixed by his remarkable transformation, I narrow my eyes on him. "You do look different; I'll give you that," I add, still unsure whether to relax or run away screaming stranger danger.

"I should hope so; that sucked! I'd hate to come out looking like before. Would definitely not be worth it." He lifts his broad, significantly larger shoulders and now muscular arms high over his head and stretches his back and neck from side to side, his vertebra popping into place with several loud cracks.

"Do you feel different?" I ask.

"I guess so. Stronger, maybe." With a flex of his bicep, the sleeves of his t-shirt rip in several places. "Oops."

We both laugh quietly.

"Looks like someone needs to go shopping!" I say with a chuckle. "I just happen to know of someone dying to get out of this place and would love to take you in a heartbeat."

"No way, not gonna happen. She'll make me wear girly colors." He cringes. "Finn might be okay with pink, but uh-uh, not this guy," he adds as he removes the ruined shirt and tosses it in the wastebasket by the door.

I laugh, knowing how right he is.

"Shae, this is fun and all, and don't take this the wrong way or anything, but what are you doing in here?"

"Wha—I wanted to make sure you were ok!"

"Really?"

"Yes. *Really!* What, you think I came in here to drool all over you?" I scoff. "I didn't even know what to expect." I growl playfully, shoving him to the side, "Sheesh, please, get over yourself. And move over." I grin and plop down beside him on the bed.

"Alright, alright, no need to get violent," he says, sitting back up. "Actually, I thought maybe you came to show me that gigantic rock on your finger." He grins and nods to my hand. "Sorry, I missed the big moment. How'd it go?"

I give him a side glance of annoyance as I fiddle with the ring, finding it strange to wear a ring on my finger after so long.

"Oh right, the howl. Well, anyway, I guess congratulations are in order."

"Thanks," I say quietly.

Hearing Niall's new voice throws me off for a second. It's so hard to believe he's changed so much.

"Hey, how'd Jamie take it? I bet she flipped out,

right?" He says eagerly with his eyebrows raised high.

"She would have, but she was too worried about Finn, and by the time everyone showed back up, it was too late."

"Well, that just sucks."

"Meh, it wasn't a good time anyway," I confirm with a false smile. "Never seems to be nowadays, does it?"

He grimaces. "Definitely does suck, that's fer sure," he says softly. "So, now that it's official, how are you feeling about accepting Marcas's proposal after, you know, the Jared fiasco?"

I manage a large smile because, for the first time in a very long time, my heart doesn't ache with regret when I hear Jared's name.

"Well." he laughs. "I'll take that to mean you're happy about it! Guess it also means no more moping around the house for you." He adds with a mischievous grin, eyes full of playful taunting.

"Funny." I glare as I elbow him in the ribs and then wince as I rub the pain away. "And I wasn't moping."

He starts to laugh loudly, then quickly covers his mouth, his eyes wide when I shush him.

We then laugh some more but keep it contained in our mouths.

"Seriously though," Niall says, finally catching his breath, his smile fading. "I can't believe Conall ruined your moment."

"Yeah, talk about horrible timing."

"No joke, those howls were deafening. Talk about heartache."

"Niall, that's not funny."

"I'm serious; I'm thinking we've underestimated Conall's feelings for you."

I swallow hard, trying to hold my nauseated stomach in check. I knew Marcas and Korin were downplaying the magnitude of the situation with Conall. Even Niall sees the danger in what we now face; a heartbroken, angry, psychotic, lovesick, probably homicidal—definitely stalker—maniac who can't and won't take me not choosing him as final.

My pajamas, suddenly feeling two sizes too small, grow warm. I cough and pull at the collar, trying to catch my breath.

"Uh, you don't look so good!"

"You think?" I heave as my chest tightens.

"Dang it! Stop saying every stupid thing that pops into your head, ya idiot!" he says, hitting himself in the head. "I'm so sorry, Shae."

"I know." I exhale deeply, the air finally reaching my lungs again.

"Goes to show, brawn doesn't always accompany brains," he says, discontented.

I smile because he sure is enormous now. "It's not your fault," I say, patting his knee. "You stated the

231

obvious, which is now the story of my life."

A quick knock comes at the door as it slowly opens. "Shae, you in here?" Marcas whispers, knowing very well I am.

"She's right here," Niall mumbles.

"What are you two doing? It's kind of late," he says as he enters the room and leans his elbow on the corner of the dresser by the door.

"Sorry. We were just talking. Did we wake you?" I ask.

He shrugs and ruffles his hair with his hand as he yawns. "Not really."

"I couldn't sleep. Had to check on him," I say, bumping shoulders with Niall, who has been examining his flexed biceps in the shadows of the dim lamp. "As you can see, he's all better," I add, rolling my eyes, but he is too preoccupied with himself to see.

"Good to see you're still alive, little brother," Marcas says, his face beaming.

Niall sits up straight, thrusts his fists onto his waist, and widens his puffed-out chest while showing off his muscular stature as he lifts his chin proudly like a superhero.

"Like to see Sam and Finn try to punch me now!"

"My money's on you." I laugh.

Marcas chuckles lightheartedly as he watches me cautiously. I know he must have sensed my anxiety attack.

"Come on; let's leave the egotist to his narcissism." I grin as I stand up.

"Hah, you know you love me!" Niall heckles.

"You're lucky I do," I jeer back, shoving away the leg he'd just tried to kick me with.

Walking to the door, I then kiss Marcas before smiling back at Niall. "I'm glad you're not dead, too," I whisper roughly and grin smugly before closing the door as he switches off the lamp.

CHAPTER 13

Let It Begin.

With a snarl on my face and a heavy huff, I aggressively flip the steaming pancake, splattering batter as it lands on the edge of the griddle. The three I'd already cooked are charred and inedible on a plate beside me.

Outside, Finn chants, "Faster, faster," as the others cheer and laugh. Annoyance instantly takes me over.

First thing this morning, all the guys had wanted to go out front to see how much Niall's new body could handle, wanting me to cook in their stead. What are we, back in the Stone Age?

"Come on! You don't want Niall to starve, do

you?" Sam had said with sparkles in his eyes. "He burned like a million calories last night. You see him; he needs sustenance!"

"So! Why do I have to be the one to do it?"

"Because you're awesome like that." Sam winked and smiled wide.

I had wanted to say no out of spite, but it was Niall we were talking about, and a part of me worried he really was that hungry.

I could have just waited to make the food, but I knew Jamie would leave for work soon. I had tried to convince her when we talked earlier not to go, but we got distracted by the ring on my finger.

"What's that like a million carrots?" she squealed. "Come on, let me try it on!"

But even with a combo of lotion and dish soap, it would not budge from my finger as if protected by some sort of supernatural defense mechanism to keep from falling off my finger or being taken without consent. I even tried to verbally give Jamie permission to try it on, but to no avail. Ultimately, she had to settle for gawking at it from the safety of my finger.

Of course, moments later, she was out the door with the others, leaving me to cook alone.

From the side window in the living room, I had watched Sam force Niall to do as many push-ups as possible with Ardan sitting on his back. They added Finn when it appeared too easy for him. I heard Jamie chanting the count, stopping at 150. Finn moved Niall on to endurance instead, making him hold the cement guards from the driveway stacked five high in his arms as he ran around the yard's perimeter.

Six scorched pancakes later, and I am forced to pay attention to breakfast rather than what's happening outside.

"Ow Ow Ow!" Jamie calls as if she's right outside the window.

Under my breath, I grumble more and jab another pancake with the spatula, then flip it over.

"Woo hoo, dang, bro, you've got strength!" I hear Finn howl.

What are they even doing?

On my tiptoes, I try to peer out the far window and down into the yard, but I can't even see past the balcony.

"Can't they just do it later so I can watch?" I grumble as I flip the latest excuse for a pancake into the garbage, along with the others on the plate.

Looking at the clock, I sigh. Forty-five minutes till Jamie leaves.

Though still vexed, I get to work with a new sense of purpose.

Just as I am placing the plate of steaming hot, perfectly golden flapjacks on the counter next to the pan of bacon and sausages, a pitcher of orange juice, and cute little glass juice cups, the door to the outside opens. Soon after, a rumble of voices comes down the hall.

Tax trods into the room and over to a warm, sunny spot on the rug by the window, where he circles twice before lying down.

"Impressive, Niall, but you still have a lot of catching up to do," Sam says as he, Niall, Ardan, and Finn file into the kitchen. "Smells delish! Thanks, Mom," he adds, smiling at me as he reaches for a piece of bacon.

Faster than he can react, I slap the back of his hand with the spatula and smile smugly.

"Not cool," he glowers, wincing in pain.

"Sorry, can't eat till we're all here," I say.

"Oh, man, I'm starving!" Finn whines, gripping his belly.

Jamie steps into the kitchen and flashes him a disappointed look, to which he responds with a guilty smile, then blows her a kiss of apology. She playfully catches it and then plops on the couch by the window.

"Boys!" Marcas calls from the hall, his voice light in tone but stern just the same.

Muffled apologies come from all of them now around the table.

"If anyone eats first, it should be Niall. Torturing him for your own pleasure." Marcas frowns, a shadow of teasing in his eyes. "Which, by the way, none of you handled so well when you first changed." He shifts his

237

gaze purposely at Finn and then Sam.

"Good morning, Mo Chroi. Breakfast smells divine," Marcas says as he sucks bacon grease from his fingers with a smack.

Threatening to swat his hand, I scowl at him playfully, "How did you get that?"

He shrugs and winks.

"Alright, dig in," I call, shaking my head at Marcas' smug grin.

They all rush the counter. Jamie keeps trying to get food, but like a skittish puppy, she pulls away when the boys grab it out from under her.

"Oh my gosh, you animals, let Jamie get some food, too!" I order, pushing a plate toward Niall. He takes it and smiles before offering a pancake to Jamie.

After piling food on their plates, the boys sit back at the table. Finn saves a seat for Jamie, who joins him soon after.

Scurrying past us, Tate grabs a plate and loads it with several pancakes and two sausage links before sitting on the loveseat.

While they all eat, I watch Jamie. As the moments tick down to when she leaves, the anxious feelings turning inside my gut worsen.

"Jamie will be fine, Shae," Marcas says, pulling me close. "Ardan can handle things."

While flipping another pancake, I whisper, "Maybe, but I don't like her being so exposed. Conall

238

knows where she works."

Marcas kisses my cheek, then moves around the counter for food. "Hey, listen up," he shouts, grabbing a few pancakes, sausage links, and a glass of juice. "I want to talk about Tynan."

A hush falls over the room.

"He's out," Marcas says flatly. "Doesn't believe Conall or his followers are enough of a threat to send reinforcements."

"Seriously?" Niall says with a mouth full of food.

"What followers?" Finn grumbles.

"Rogan, Tavis, and Luc?" Sam chimes in. "I'd hardly call that an army."

"Who's Luc?" I ask.

Niall snorts, "Conall's youngest brother."

"He was there at the rodeo in Anaconda," Finn says.

"But I wouldn't call him a warrior of any sort," Sam huffs.

"There's more," Korin says, setting his cup back on the table. "Loads more. We cannot underestimate his numbers."

"Then why won't Tynan help us?" I ask, fixing my own plate of food.

"He doesn't see it as his fight." Korin frowns.

Everyone at the table erupts in protest.

"Even with what happened the last two nights?" Niall's voice rings over the others, hushing the room.

239

"I'm sure it wouldn't change his mind either way. Tynan's spies confirmed our suspicions, yet he would not yield," Marcas adds as he fidgeted with the syrup bottle before pouring a steady stream on his pancakes. "It took a lot of convincing for him to even agree to allow Korin, Ardan, and Tate to remain here."

"But doesn't Conall's takeover threaten Tynan as much as it does us?" I ask before taking a bite of food.

"Yes," Marcas says, his voice heavy with concern. "But he doesn't think the corruption will reach his borders. And even if it did, he'd be strong enough to overthrow it. He doesn't see how easy it would be to infiltrate his lands and take over from within. He's blind to the changes happening and refuses to believe they can affect him. No offense, Korin."

"No, you're absolutely right. Father thinks he's safe from Conall's depravity if he stays out of it; however, I disagree," Korin says, rising from his seat on the couch and walking to the kitchen sink, placing his plate in it. "To evolve in this century, we must adapt. We can't allow corruption and outright rebellion to influence those around us and do nothing when we witness it. We need to stick together and work to fortify our borders."

A rumble of agreement shifts around the room.

Korin then looks at me and smiles. "Don't worry, I'm not done trying. I won't stop until he understands the huge threat we face."

240

I smile back at him, thankful for his support even if his father disapproves.

"Korin, use caution. I don't want to cause contention between any of us," Marcas says.

"Noted," Korin says respectfully.

"Ok, if not men, then what *do* we have?" Niall asks as he shoves a fork full of bacon and pancakes in his mouth.

"The mighty Marcas!" Ardan booms with pride. Having been silent until now, I almost forgot he was here. "The wisest leader of our time; his strategic skills and warrior stealth will surely lead us to victory." Ardan gives a broad smile that appears genuine but flickers with a slight sarcastic twinkle. And his words, meant to uplift and encourage, feel as if they are weighed down with mockery instead of praise. At least to me, they do.

Marcas doesn't seem to notice and nods at Ardan, then continues, "We have the greatest chance at victory because we fight for what's noble and good." Glancing at me, he smiles.

"Yeah, good always beats evil," Niall adds triumphantly. "Every time!"

"How can you possibly guarantee your victory by simply stating who is good and who is evil?" Tate questions.

The room goes dead silent.

"If Conall and his men believe what they fight for

241

is just and deserved, how can you gage whose gestures are nobler? Which is good and which is evil?" Tate asks, putting a fork full of food in his mouth.

He hadn't bothered looking at anyone as he spoke, but it was apparent he had been listening intently since most of the food on his plate had hardly been touched.

Marcas' body goes tense. "They fight for revenge, hoping to destroy our family's legacy!" He points his finger at Tate with the hand gripping the fork. "Your legacy! There's nothing noble about that."

"But what of his promises of a free future?" Tate says sharply.

"Conall doesn't give a damn about anything except tearing down tradition and giving himself the power to rule over all, to let anarchy govern our people. Does that sound like a free future that will bring anything good to our kingdom?" Marcas says with a hint of bitterness.

"I guess it depends on what side of the coin you're looking at."

"Is there something you wish to tell us, brother?" Korin warns, turning to face Tate. His demeanor remains calm, but his right hand is fisted at his side.

"Ignore him. He's baiting you," Ardan says smugly as he narrows his eyes in disgust at Tate. "Trying to cause confusion and mayhem to an already tense situation."

242

"Figures; let the cunning brother twist my words yet again," Tate mumbles.

"What did you say?" Ardan hisses, sending his chair toppling backward as he catapults out of his seat, causing a scared Tax to scurry out from under the table and rush down the hall.

Korin stretches out his arms, keeping Ardan from getting any closer to Tate, who has also stood.

"You heard me," Tate barks. "But it doesn't matter, does it? You always have a quick retort on your tongue, there to spit out whenever I have something to say! No one ever understands what I'm trying to say because you never let me explain myself."

"It's because you're full of lies, Tate," Ardan says, his words saturated with bitterness. "Korin already knows this, and Father knows better than to listen to the likes of a son, who, from birth, has never once stood by his side to fight for him."

Swallowing hard, I look at Tate, my heart aching a little for him. No one deserves such a brutal verbal lashing, let alone in front of everyone.

"You know damn well Father doesn't need me; he has the two of you," Tate yells. "Besides, you continuously twist my intentions into acts of defiance and betrayal and whisper outlandish lies to them about me."

"Tate, you're a thorn in our father's side, a blemish to our good name," Ardan growls contemptuously.

243

"You will never *say* anything worth listening to because you'll never *be* worth listening to. You continue to be a disappointment. And the only reason you're still around is because even with Father's repeated attempts to convince Mother you're not worth the hassle, she still wants you with us."

Tate's face turns beet red. "That's not true!" he screams, grabbing for Ardan.

Caught off guard, Ardan stumbles back a step. Marcas drops his plate, clutches Tate firmly by the arms, and swerves him away. Korin does the same to Ardan.

Tate flings himself free of Marcas. His troubled eyes meet mine as he storms from the room. I don't just see anger in them but heartbreak and pain.

The walls shake when the door slams hard behind him as he leaves the house.

Hatred runs far deeper than what has just played out, and my heart hurts. I feel Tate's pain as if it were my own.

No doubt Tate's behavior can be harsh and abrasive, but I have also witnessed his softer side. I do not believe it is a ruse. Even from our first conversation, I can see how his convoluted words could easily be manipulated according to one's perspective. But I also do not really know him and cannot wholeheartedly trust he isn't part of the threat we face. Not entirely, anyway, and it troubles me greatly.

"I apologize for the outbursts of my brothers," Korin says as he picks up the fallen chair and sits in it.

"Don't apologize for him, Korin," Ardan barks as he returns to the table, fixing his messed-up hair. "They have eyes; they can see who's at fault." He smiles at Jamie and then over her shoulder at me like he wants to ensure we've been watching the whole thing.

I find his need for an audience appalling.

Gentle chimes sound from Jamie's cell on the counter. I hand it to her, and she shuts it off.

"I do, however, feel great remorse for letting his childish behavior ruin your fantastically prepared breakfast and hope you'll forgive me," Ardan says stiffly to me before turning his attention back to Jamie. "Come, let's get you to work. I don't wish you to be late on my account." He finishes the last piece of pancake on his plate and moves to help her from the table.

"I hate that you have to go," I say to Jamie as I anxiously twist the towel in my hands. "Keep your cell on you the whole time, ok."

"I'll be fine," she says, putting her plate in the sink. "And home before you know it." She then hugs me. "Now, let me see that rock one last time." Grinning, she grabs my hand and smiles wide. "So gorgeous!" Then she tries to take it off.

245

"Alright, already," I tease, taking my hand back. "And I mean it; text me, ok?"

Giving a single nod of assurance, she grabs her purse, then turns and tosses me a warm smile before following Ardan outside.

A pit of unease forms in my stomach as I watch her go. I don't care how confident she is about Ardan's abilities; I am way more concerned about the crazy, lovesick, would-be king, wolfguy out there capable of causing a great deal of trouble for us if he wants to. And according to Niall, Conall is capable of a whole heap of it and much more.

*　*　*

The horrible feeling comes without warning, like a cheap one-two punch to my gut.

Having just taken a bite of my sandwich, I spit it out, cough, and gasp for breath as I watch Ardan hobble across the yard alone.

"Ardan, what are you doing here?" Marcas asks sharply.

"Wh-where's Jamie?" I stammer, feeling the color drain from my face.

Ardan's chin trembles. "Shae, I'm so sorry."

My body wobbles; everything starts to spin. Marcas catches me before I hit the ground. Gently lowering me into a chair under the deck, he looks at

Ardan again.

"Marcas, you've got to believe me; there was nothing I could do!"

Marcas' eyes narrow, anger peeking through. "What happened?"

"I mean, I-I don't know what happened," Ardan says, panicked, though his eyes don't seem to match his emotion. "All I saw was a delivery driver arguing with Jamie's boss. Then, someone must have struck me from behind because when I came to, I was tied up, my phone was gone, and so was Jamie."

My chest, heavy without breath, burns as my heart races out of control. "How could you let this happen?" I scream as I scramble toward Ardan. "How could you?"

While Marcas gently puts me back in the chair, Ardan cowers away, his face contorted in utter shock at my hostility.

Kneeling down, Marcas puts his hands on my face. "Shae—Shae listen to me," he says sternly when I try to force his hands away hysterically. "Please, look at me!"

I shut my eyes, scrunching so tight no light can get in. Tears stream down my cheeks.

"I knew something bad would happen; I just knew it!" I sob even harder, imagining how scared Jamie must be. "We never should have let her go!"

"Shae, I need you to open your eyes!" Marcas says

again, worry in his voice.

"No!" I shake my head. "I can't." Please, someone rid me of this nightmare!

"Mo Chroi, please," Marcas whispers again. "I'm sure he didn't mean for this to happen."

My eyes pop open. Through my tears, I glare past Marcas at Ardan. "Why didn't you protect her?"

Ardan shakes his head fervently. "I tried," he moans.

My fingernails dig into my palms as I clutch them into tight fists. But I do not move to strike.

Marcas kisses my forehead and gets to his feet.

Half a second later, Niall runs down the stairs, skipping several at a time and somehow avoiding pummeling into Marcas at the bottom step. At the same time, Sam, Finn, and Korin come sprinting from the back of the house.

From their sudden presence, I can only assume Marcas must have called them telepathically.

"What happened now?" Sam asks with a pinch of annoyance. When he sees Ardan, he stops short. "What's he doing here?"

Seeing me, Niall runs to my side. "Shae, you ok?"

Finn suddenly grabs Ardan and shoves him against the post supporting the above deck. "What do you mean Jamie's gone?"

"Conall took her!" I cry.

"No!" Finn screams in Ardan's face. "How could

248

they? You were watching her!"

Marcas removes Finn's clenched hands from Ardan, who immediately stumbles away.

"Finn, I know you're upset, but—"

Finn shoves Marcas away angrily, his nostrils flaring, and punches the wood post where Ardan has been standing before. Red blood seeps from the cracks in his knuckles.

"Finn!" Marcas warns. "I need you to be level-headed! Conall is counting on you getting fired up like this."

Finn's eyes burn with fury at Marcas. "Then stop standing around and do something! Find her! Get her back!"

"We will, Finn!" Marcas says firmly, then looks at me with assurance, yet worry remains in his eyes. "I promise!"

To be continued . . .

249

BOOK 3

Here is a sneak peek into

DECEPTION BY NIGHTFALL

the next installment in the

SECRETS BY MOONLIGHT SAGA

—"She must be so scared," I say, fighting back more worry.

Marcas caresses my knuckle with his thumb and gives me a weary smile. His eyes focus on mine as though doing so will hypnotize me into calmness. They are definitely gorgeous to look at, but nowhere near pervasive enough to fix the level of anxiety and dread I now feel.

"We found trails all over, but they crisscrossed with old ones, muddying the scent," Marcas says, looking at the others. "It was almost too difficult to decipher which direction they were going."

"But not impossible," Niall chimes in.

"Lucky for us, Niall's transformation happened when it did. His sense of smell is like nothing I've ever encountered."

"I picked up on the trail just past the dirt road at the park." Niall grins. "They were headed toward Granite's Ghost Town. Now we have to figure out how to get in, get Jamie, and get out without someone spotting us."

"We take them by surprise," Sam says, wiping his hands with a napkin. "Use a diversion and strike when they're distracted!"

"Divide and surround them," Finn argues.

"But we don't know how many of them there are," Korin says. "It would be done with great risk."

"Are you nuts? There's too many of us to sneak in undetected. We might as well walk in and hand ourselves over!" Finn says.

"But it's still better than the alternative," Niall counters.

"We'll have more of a fighting chance if we stick together." Marcas kisses my hand, then releases it, letting it fall to my side as he begins to pace the room with Finn. "I'm thinking more of a covert operation. Maybe send in Korin, Finn, and Sam to get a head count. See how many of them we're dealing with. Then get word to the rest of us. That way, our numbers are small, but Tate, Niall, and I would be right behind, ready to proceed as planned."

2

"Sounds viable," Korin says with optimism.

"Beats sitting around here," Finn growls.

"Wait a minute," I say, stepping forward. "What about me? Wh-Who do I go with?"

In an upheaval, I hear all at once, "No, it's too dangerous," and "You can't go!", "No, she should go. It's not safe to stay!", "Are you crazy? You want her to get killed?" and so on, to the point I can't tell anymore who's saying what.

The sharp sting of anger rises inside me.

"Geeze, why don't you just tell me how you really feel?" I snap back, which produces more incoherent arguing from the boys.

I look at Marcas for a sign he agrees with me, and I believe I get my answer with his pressed smile.

"All right, enough!" Marcas thunders. The room goes silent.

Confident in what he's about to say, I prepare for my triumph with a significant smile.

"Shae, you're not going, and that's final."

"Wait, what? I thought—"

He shakes his head.

Heat rushes me like I'm standing in front of an open oven. "You can't stop me from going. No way am I watching everyone I love run off without me *again*!"

"Shae, it's too dangerous. There's no way."

My lungs burn, heavy with every aggressive breath. "Marcas, please don't do this. Not again!"

3

"I can't let you come," he says a bit softer, but his eyes still hold firm with control.

The amulet, resting under my shirt, warms against my skin. It calls to me. I pull it out and hold it high. "What about this? If it makes me a wolf, it means I'm one of you. You have to take me. I'm stronger than you think. I can help. Please!"

Marcas sighs, his eyes narrowing in conflicting thoughts. "I—"

"Shae's right." Sam smiles at me. "She stood up to Conall and held her own. I was angry before, so I didn't notice, but she's strong."

I gawk at him in utter shock. After what I put him through, Sam was the last person I figured would sway my way. But I'm glad he's on my side.

"Marcas, this is madness." Niall rises from the armchair. "You know as well as I do, the battlefield is no place for a—"

"A what?" I glare. "A girl? Is that what you were going to say? I'm a girl, so what? Doesn't mean I can't fight. Teach me. I can take care of myself!"

"I was about to say human, but whatever," Niall mumbles.

I watch Finn shake his head, agreeing with Marcas and Niall, and it makes my insides boil.

"Thanks a lot, Finn," I say sourly. He doesn't bother to hide his eye roll as he looks away.

4

His reaction would hurt more if not for the rapid inferno raging inside me. Jamie's gone, and I'll be damned if I'm gonna let them force me out of the rescue.—

STEPHANIE L. MCMULLIN

Having had an overactive imagination since birth, Stephanie has finally put her creativity to print. *Secrets By Moonlight* was her first solo published work of fiction, followed by book two, *Fate By Sunrise*. Look for the exciting continuation of the saga in *Deception By Nightfall* to be released in 2024. Stephanie resides in Spanish Fork, Utah, with her husband and four children.

www.ingramcontent.com/pod-product-compliance
Lightning Source LLC
Chambersburg PA
CBHW020054180626
46812CB00006B/2326